Dear Reader,

When I approached writing my book based on
The Little Mermaid, I couldn't help but think of
all of us out there who long for experiences and
adventures that seem just beyond our reach.
I imagined a girl, sitting alone on a rock in the
middle of the ocean, staring at the bright lights
of a land she cannot go to. My mermaid is that
person who finds not only the adventures she's
been seeking, but the man of her dreams! Not,
I might add, without a few obstacles thrown in
along the way!

I hope you enjoy reading this book as much as I
enjoyed writing it.

Cathy

Once Upon a Temptation

Will they live passionately ever after?

Once upon a time, in a land far, far away, there was a billionaire—or eight! Each billionaire had riches beyond your wildest imagination. Still, they were each missing something: love. But the path to true love is never easy...even if you're one of the world's richest men!

Inspired by fairy tales like *Beauty and the Beast* and *Little Red Riding Hood*, the Once Upon a Temptation collection will take you on a passion-filled journey of ultimate escapism.

Fall in love with...

Cinderella's Royal Secret by Lynne Graham

Beauty and Her One-Night Baby by Dani Collins

Shy Queen in the Royal Spotlight
by Natalie Anderson

Claimed in the Italian's Castle by Caitlin Crews

Expecting His Billion-Dollar Scandal
by Cathy Williams

Taming the Big Bad Billionaire by Pippa Roscoe

The Flaw in His Marriage Plan by Tara Pammi

His Innocent's Passionate Awakening
by Melanie Milburne

Cathy Williams

—

EXPECTING HIS BILLION-DOLLAR SCANDAL

HARLEQUIN

PRESENTS

Recycling programs for this product may not exist in your area.

ISBN-13: 978-1-335-14861-2

Expecting His Billion-Dollar Scandal

For questions and comments about the quality of this book, please contact us at CustomerService@Harlequin.com.

Harlequin Enterprises ULC
22 Adelaide St. West, 40th Floor
Toronto, Ontario M5H 4E3, Canada
www.Harlequin.com

Printed in U.S.A.

Cathy Williams can remember reading Harlequin books as a teenager, and now that she is writing them, she remains an avid fan. For her, there is nothing like creating romantic stories and engaging plots, and each and every book is a new adventure. Cathy lives in London, and her three daughters—Charlotte, Olivia and Emma—have always been, and continue to be, the greatest inspirations in her life.

To my supportive children and my partner, David,
who has been a huge source of inspiration.

CHAPTER ONE

'WHERE AM I?'

Cordelia swung around and stared at the man lying on the bed. He hadn't spoken for three days. He'd drifted in and out of sleep, as Dr Greenway had predicted he would. He'd opened his eyes and stared around him but in the unfocused way of someone not really taking anything in.

'Keep him on liquids,' the doctor had advised, 'but there's nothing a hospital can do for him that you can't. Less, probably. You know how overworked and understaffed they are there, especially with half of it closed for renovations. The man wouldn't get much of a look-in. As it stands, he must be as strong as an ox to have endured what he has without being the worse for wear.'

So she'd settled him in one of the spare bedrooms in the rambling house she shared with her father, and together they had taken turns keeping their eye on him, relying on the doctor's twice-daily visits for reassurance that a sudden spiral downwards wasn't on the cards. He was roused for his liquid intake and, in the past twenty-four hours, had managed to eat two light meals. Her father had shown him the bathroom and changed him into some of his own clothes.

He had been making progress but, really, he'd still been out of it. Until now.

She stared at him and her heart sped up.

Luca. That was the man's name. Luca Baresi. She knew that because she'd found his wallet in his trousers and had searched for a name and any sort of contact number she could possibly find so that she could notify a member of his family about the accident.

His identity was all she could come up with. God knew, he'd been blown about on the waves long enough for the water to claim his mobile phone, had he been carrying one. The contents of the wallet, which had been wedged in his trouser pocket, had largely been too sodden and waterlogged to prove helpful.

'Well?'

Cordelia blinked and walked towards him. He was propping himself up against the pillow, staring at her, eyes narrowed, head tilted questioningly to one side.

It had been one thing absently admiring the man's striking good looks when he'd been more or less out of it. It felt quite different now, with his green eyes arrowing onto her with laser-like intensity.

'You're in my father's house.' She hovered next to the bed and then gingerly sat on the side.

Eyes as green as the ocean when the sun blazed down on it, she thought distractedly, and the sort of bronzed complexion of someone who definitely didn't hark from Cornish shores. Even the guys she knew, fishermen like her dad, were pale in comparison.

'What am I doing in your father's house and why am I wearing these clothes?'

'Don't you remember anything?'

'I recall being in my boat.' He frowned. 'One minute the sun was shining and the next minute, the sky had turned black.'

Cordelia was nodding sympathetically while thinking how fantastic his voice was, as deep and as rich as the darkest of chocolate. Very distracting.

'That's the weather for you here,' she murmured. 'Especially at this time of year. You'd think summer might be predictable but a storm can erupt out of nowhere.' She gazed at his hand. He was massaging his collarbone, still frowning, trying to get his thoughts together. Understandable, given what he'd been through. He really was, she thought, stupidly good-looking with that dark, dark hair and olive skin and features chiselled with breathtaking perfection.

Or maybe, at the ripe old age of twenty-four and stuck out here, living a life as predictable as the rising and setting of the sun, she was just easily impressed by someone halfway decent.

She stared at him from under lowered lashes and thought that this guy was far from halfway decent. Halfway decent had been Barry, the guy she had dated for eight months before finally admitting to herself that they were never going to get anywhere and certainly not between the sheets, which, as he had implied with ever increasing clarity, was the destination he had had his eyes on and never mind the business of romance and a courtship to get there. Some straggly flowers and the occasional movie or night out at the local pub, had been top of his game when it had come to wooing her.

'That's obviously what happened to you.' She cleared her throat and fidgeted because he was staring at her with such intensity. 'Three days ago. You should have checked the weather report before you decided to go sailing. Most people around here do. They know how unpredictable the weather can be but you're not from around here, are you?'

'What are you doing here?'

'I beg your pardon?'

'Are you a nurse?'

'No. I…no, I'm not. I suppose you're wondering why you're here and not in a hospital, but the local hospital is tiny and Dr Greenway didn't think it necessary to have you taken by ambulance over to the next biggest hospital, which is quite some distance away. He said you would recover just fine here when I called him over. After I found you.'

'You found me?'

'I happened to be looking out of my bedroom window at the time.'

Staring off into the distance and thinking about what it must be like to live out there…in the big, bad world…where adventures happened and the people you met weren't the same people you went to school with when you were five…where excitement lay behind half-opened doors and sadness and loss were no longer her faithful companions…

She blushed because, although he didn't say anything, she got the weird feeling that he knew just what was going through her head, which, of course, was impossible.

'Your boat was just a speck in the distance being tossed around in the storm.'

'At which point you…?'

'Dad wasn't around,' she said bluntly. 'And I'm as confident on the water as anyone else I know.' She saw his eyebrows shoot up and her mouth thinned in a defensive line. She knew nothing about the stranger lying on the bed but she knew enough to realise that, given his staggering good looks and an air of confidence that couldn't be concealed even wearing her father's weathered clothes, he wouldn't be short of female company. And the female company wouldn't, she was thinking, be the sort capable of sailing the high seas in stormy weather.

'Are you, now?'

'Better, probably.' She shrugged. 'I got my captain's licence when I was eighteen and I have every qualification needed to fish at sea. I know everything there is to know about sea survival, including what to do if there's a fire at sea, and I have brilliant first-aid skills.'

'So you rescued me because I was stupid enough to get behind the wheel of my boat without first checking the weather forecast. How did you manage to do that?'

'I used the fastest and most robust boat from my father's collection and headed out. It didn't occur to me to ask anyone for help. I knew that if someone was on the boat and in trouble, then aid had to be immediate.'

'I am remiss in not thanking you. I remember taking the boat out and I remember the storm rolling in but after that...'

'You were out of it. I know. You were in the water clinging to the side of your boat when I got to you. Semi-conscious.'

'And yet you managed to haul me into your own boat.'

Cordelia thought of all those dainty five-foot-nothings she had always longed to be. Fragile and delicate, demanding the adoring attention of boys who had always seemed genetically geared to leap into the protective mode the second they came near.

She'd never been one of those. She was five ten and sinewy. She could swim like a fish and sail with the best of them and it showed in the strong lines of her body.

'You weren't completely out of it,' she muttered. 'You easily helped yourself. Getting back in one piece was a far bigger problem with the storm kicking up a gear and the waves big enough to take us both under.'

'But you never answered my question. Why are you here?'

Cordelia shot him a puzzled frown. 'I told you. I work here. With my father. I help run his business. He owns eight boats. He fishes but also does a rental business to subsidise his income.'

'A challenging life for a young girl.' The green eyes were curious and assessing.

Now she knew what he was getting at. Why was she here? Was that what was going through his head? Instead of living it up in a city somewhere? With a boyfriend and a giddy round of parties and clubs? Doing all those things girls her age did? Nearly all of her friends had disappeared off to university somewhere and those who had returned had all, without exception, had a boyfriend in tow. They'd married and had their first child within the year. They'd had their fun and had chosen to return to the village to settle down because they loved it here.

That option had not been on the table for her and it was why that big world out there seemed so full of possibilities. Possibilities that would never be explored but which she yearned for anyway.

She chose to interpret his remark at face value because her life was none of his business and he certainly wasn't to know that he'd struck a nerve.

'The sea can be very challenging. But it can also be very rewarding.'

A brief and telling silence greeted this remark.

'I should introduce myself,' he said.

'No need.'

'How's that?'

'I know who you are.'

'You know who I am…'

She noted the way he stiffened, the way his face became shuttered, his fabulous eyes veiled. She had no idea what was going through his head but to dispel the sudden tension, she smiled.

'Luca. Luca Baresi. I'm sorry but when I brought you back here, and after you were examined by the doctor, I felt I should see if I could find some form of identification so that I could let your loved ones know where you were.'

'You went through my stuff.'

'There wasn't much to go through,' Cordelia told him quickly. 'Trust me, it was the last thing I wanted to do but I don't imagine you would have thanked me if you'd come to and found that no one could be bothered to try and discover who you were! Everything was unreadable because of the sea water but your identification card was plastic-coated and I managed to make out your name. If you're up to it, I can bring you the telephone and you can call your… family. They must be worried sick about you. Where do you live?'

'I'm not from around here.'

'Further inland?' She nodded thoughtfully. 'Lots of people descend from London in the summer months and lots of them have second homes in some of the more popular towns. They can't bear to be too far away from gastropubs and fancy restaurants.'

'You don't like that?'

'I don't care one way or another,' she said honestly. 'Tourism is great when it comes to renting boats, as it happens, but I'm pretty much the only person around here who thinks like that. If you're close enough, I dare say my dad can drive you back to your wife and kids.'

'Wife and kids? What makes you think I'm married?'

'I…' Her heart fluttered and she could feel the hot burn of colour in her cheeks. 'I suppose I just assumed…'

'Are *you* married?'

'No.'

'Strangely enough, I would have assumed that you were.'

'Why?' Her skin was tingling all over. Her eyes were drawn to his but once there, she was finding it impossible to look away, and something inside her shied away from the notion that he might sum her up and write her off as a country bumpkin, bowled over by his excessive good looks.

So she glanced right past him to the view outside the window of the bedroom, one of swirling clouds and pale grey skies and a drizzle that hadn't stopped ever since she'd rescued him from those stormy waters. Summer had gone into temporary retreat and she had no idea when it planned on returning. Just something else about living in this part of the world.

'You're young,' he drawled lightly. 'You're attractive. How is it that you haven't been snapped up by some local eligible bachelor? Maybe you've just returned from university? Still finding your feet back in the family home?'

'Not everyone has had the opportunity to go to university, Mr Baresi.' Her voice had dropped a few degrees and her violet eyes were cool when they rested on his face.

She'd had plans. She'd had her dreams but life and fate had managed to get in the way of her fulfilling those dreams.

She wondered whether things would have been different if her mother hadn't died when she'd been a kid. Mown down by a speeding car in London on one of her rare shopping trips. Her father had closed so many doors afterwards. He had become paranoid about her leaving the safety and security of the village. If she ventured into one of the bigger towns, he'd wait by the window for her, even when, at the age of ten, she'd gone in a gang with one of her friends' parents. School outings had been a nightmare because she'd known that he would be back at the house, trying hard to quell his anxiety. A skiing trip at the age of fourteen had been out of the question. He'd given permission but she'd seen the fear in his eyes and she'd quietly turned down the opportunity. She had learnt to support her father but, in doing so, had continued to carry both their pain on her shoulders. His fear was a constant reminder of their loss.

Even so…even with all that, university had beckoned and she had known that, for both their sakes, it was something she wanted and needed to do.

When she was seventeen, having been accepted at her first choice of university in Exeter, which, she had assured her dad, was only a hop and a skip away, both their lives had been shattered by the death of her twin brother. Alex had been her rock, tuned into her feelings in ways that had been quiet and instinctive. He had *understood*. He had given her strength as the pattern of their lives, following the loss of their mother, had changed. He had supported her and encouraged her and fortified her because their father's fears had always seemed to revolve around *her*. The assumption was that Alex could look after himself.

Alex had had no dreams of going to university. He'd always planned on taking over the family business. Fishing was in his blood. It wasn't to be and when he died, all her dreams had been snuffed out and she had resigned herself to taking up where her brother had left off. There were times when it felt as though loss upon loss had piled up on top of her, a weight she could barely carry, with no one in whom she could confide. The carefree joys of being young had never felt within her grasp.

Not a day passed when Cordelia didn't think of the future that had turned to dust before it could even begin, but she had hunkered down, had thrown herself into the business and had proved herself an exceptional sailor. The sea became her haven. It brought her peace and out there, in the open ocean, she could let her thoughts drift and wonder what it might be like to see the world. She could swim like a fish and swimming was always a wonderful escape.

What would this swarthy stranger think were she to confide in him? she wondered.

'Being *snapped up* by some eligible local boy has never been one of my ambitions,' she retorted quickly.

Luca smiled slowly and that slow smile sent a tingle of awareness racing through her body, igniting everything in its path. Her nerves fluttered and the sudden throb between her legs, a sensual reaction that was immediate and intensely physical, shocked her to the core.

Her eyes wide, the thoughts vanished from her head in a whoosh and she stared at him for a few panicked seconds, completely blindsided by a rush of sensation unlike anything she had ever felt before.

He'd hoisted himself higher up on the bed and she subliminally took in the breadth of his shoulders and the raw physicality of his body, which, maybe, she'd subconsciously noticed before but not like this. Then again, he hadn't been addressing her before and engaging with her the way he was now.

She edged off the bed and for the first time in for ever was acutely aware of how she looked.

Faded jeans, faded grey jumper, her waist-long blonde hair pulled back into a lopsided ponytail. As always, she was bare of make-up and as tanned as she ever got from the summer sun, which was hot enough to burn when it decided to show its face. She was barefoot, as she always was when she was in the house, and she shoved her hands behind her back. They were practical hands, used to boats and ropes and the sea.

'Where are you going?'

'I have stuff to do. Work. I only came in here to check on you and refresh your glass of water.'

'You mentioned a telephone.'

'Huh?' She was backing away towards the door, wondering why she was so nervous when, in actual fact, she never was when it came to the opposite sex.

'In the absence of my mobile phone, I'll have to use your landline to make contact with…my father.'

Cordelia blinked. 'I'm sorry I couldn't find any contact numbers in your wallet,' she said in a rush. 'It must feel like an invasion of your privacy, but, like I said, I only wanted to find out who you were and who I might be able to contact to let them know about the boating accident. Your dad must be worried sick.'

'That's not entirely how my life works.'

They stared at one another for a few long, silent seconds.

She was quite stunning, Luca thought absently, and what was almost impossible to credit was the fact that she seemed so unaware of her attributes. She was tall and athletic, her body, from what he could see, sinewy and strong. It should have put him off because he had always been drawn to slight, ultra-feminine women, but it didn't. Her legs, encased in faded jeans, were long and he could detect the fullness of her rounded breasts beneath the drab jumper. Never had he seen any woman so successfully conceal every single womanly trait she might possess. Was that deliberate, he wondered, or did the fashion police patrol the streets of the village, clamping down on anything that wasn't functional?

His eyes drifted up to her oval-shaped face. Her lips were full, her nose short and straight and her eyes a shade of violet he had never seen before. But her hair...

Luca thought of the highly groomed, sophisticated women who flitted in and out of his life. The woman in front of him couldn't have been more different and her hair said it all. She had yanked it back into a ponytail that couldn't seem to quite make its mind up as to which way it should fall, but, even so, the colours were so vibrant that he couldn't drag his eyes away. Every shade of blonde was there, from platinum blonde to the rich hues of pale honey and deeper toffee. A life spent outdoors, he assumed, doing whatever it was she did out there on the high seas. Fishing and rescuing idiots who went out in boats without first having a look at the weather forecast.

He closed down wayward thoughts that suddenly shot into his head at speed. Thoughts about how she would look underneath the workman-like clothes, what that body would feel like under his exploring hands.

Such options, for a multitude of reasons, were firmly off the table.

'I will, naturally, pay you for the cost of the phone call.'

'Why would you do that?' Cordelia asked, bewil-

dered. Did he think that they intended to charge him
for his stay at the house? That they wanted money
from him? That he had to pay his way the second
he gained full consciousness, right down to the cost
of a phone call? She bristled. 'We're not the sort of
people who would think of charging you for using
the telephone,' she said coolly. 'I may have rescued
you but I didn't bring you here so that we could start
charging you for your stay.'

'The phone call will be to Italy,' Luca said drily.

'Italy?' He was Italian. She should have worked
that out for herself going by his name alone, but she
hadn't because this wasn't the sort of Cornish village that was invaded by tourists during the height
of the summer season. Outsiders were few and far
between and yet here was this striking Italian, lying
on a bed in her father's house. She felt a buzz of excitement as her imagination took flight. Italy! Just
the taste of it on her tongue felt good.

'It's where I live.' He watched her carefully from
under his lashes. He watched to see whether she
would make any connections. In Italy, his name
would be quickly recognised. Even here, in this
country, many people would have heard of the Baresi name, if only because of its association with the
wine. The House of Baresi was legendary, as was the
formidable wealth of its aristocratic family. Luca Baresi had lived his life in the spotlight of his noble an-

cestry. His social circle was huge but around it was a protective circle, a dividing line that mere mortals were seldom allowed to cross. It wasn't of his devising. It was the way it was, and if there were moments when he longed to walk out of that circle and never look back, then he was accustomed to quickly closing them down because he knew where his duties lay.

His friends, the members of his extended family—they were all, to varying degrees, as privileged as he was. To the best of his knowledge, the only commoner to have ever broken through those rigid walls had been his mother and that tale had hardly had a happy ending.

This was an avenue of thought he was, likewise, accustomed to shutting down whenever it happened to make an uninvited appearance and he did so now, with ruthless efficiency.

'Tuscany,' he offered. 'Have you been there?'

'I don't often leave Cornwall,' Cordelia admitted and she grimaced at his expression of incredulity.

She met so few people, she realised. Life was so predictable for her and yet she was still young. Twenty-four years old! She should be enjoying all sorts of new and life-changing experiences. Everyone in the village knew her back story but now, the urge to confide in someone new, someone from a faraway and exotic place that she would probably never visit, at least not in the near future, was over-powering.

'Why is that?'

He paused to look at her and she stared back at him in silence because suddenly everything, the bits and pieces and nuts and bolts of her life, seemed so overwhelming. She thought about all the things that had happened to her. All the things locking her into this one place. Keeping her there as securely as if she had been trapped in a cage. How on earth could she unpick all those pieces of her past and put them into a few casual sentences? It was crazy anyway. Forget about silly urges! She barely knew the guy. She wouldn't know where to begin when it came to answering that simple question he had asked.

He stretched and, in one swift movement, flung aside the covers and swung his legs over the side of the bed. 'I need to move around,' he threw over his shoulder, as he headed to the wardrobe and the only place his clothes could be. 'And change back into my own clothes.'

Cordelia nodded mutely, riveted to him. To start with he had more or less hobbled, hanging onto her father's arm to make his way to the bathroom, and even when, after day one, his strength had begun to resurface, he had still moved slowly, hesitantly. It was obvious that he was well on the road to rude health because his movements now were assured and graceful and captivating.

She felt that her mouth might be hanging open. Her jaw certainly dropped to the ground when, without warning and with his back still to her, he began stripping off without the slightest hint of inhibition.

She looked away. Her mouth had gone dry and she could feel the hot burn of colour suffusing her face.

'You can look now.' There was amusement in his voice a couple of minutes later and she slowly turned round to face him.

Her cheeks were still pink with embarrassment.

Her body language shrieked her discomfort. Luca had seen nothing like it before. Had there ever been a time in his life when he had been with any woman who had seen his semi-naked body and acted as though the ground would be doing her a favour if it opened and swallowed her up? He couldn't help the spurt of curiosity about her. So beautiful and yet could she possibly be as innocent as she looked?

And what about never leaving this place? How did that begin to make sense?

'How old are you?' he asked suddenly.

'Twenty-four just. Why?'

Luca shrugged. 'You say that you seldom leave here?'

'It's a beautiful part of the world. You'd be surprised how many people who live by the sea find it impossible to stray far from it.'

Not her, though. No, not her, but something inside her felt compelled to defend herself against his curiosity.

He let that non-answer go and instead looked around him. He had no recollection of being brought into the house and he hadn't spared a single second to so much as glance outside the bedroom window. He rectified that now and what he saw was a limitless view of grey sea, a ribbon of road, currently empty, and the tangle of greenery at the side of the road, stretching out towards what seemed to be a gentle incline down, he guessed, to the ocean front. Everything was shrouded in a cloud of fine, persistent drizzle. The remnants of the storm that had capsized his boat.

Then he looked around him, taking in his surroundings fully and for the first time.

Luca rarely noticed his surroundings, at least not the mansion in which he lived or any of the other expensive properties he owned. They were lavish. He knew that. But a lifetime of wealth had made him immune to their impact. Nor did he pay much attention to any of the houses in which his friends or relatives lived. They all ran along the same lines. Some were bigger than others, few more opulent. The town houses and apartments in which the various girlfriends he had had over the years lived had all been expensive, courtesy of rich parents. Such was his life.

The room in which he was standing was far from

lavish. It was large, with a wooden floor over which a worn Persian rug tried hard to add a bit of luxury. The furniture was all old but gleaming and highly polished and the walls could have done with a top-up on the paint. But the bed had been incredibly comfortable and he had to admit that there was something seductively cosy about the room, despite its lack of expensive furnishings.

'Show me around?' he heard himself ask her. 'I need to stretch my legs. I feel like I've been confined in one place for far too long.'

'What about the phone call?'

'Ah.' Green eyes met violet and Luca smiled, because it wasn't often that he was in the company of a woman who didn't know his worth. It felt strangely liberating. He could be himself. He was no longer the man who was committed to driving forward the considerable family business he now ran, having hauled it back from the brink thanks to his father. Nor was he the prized aristocrat who couldn't enter a room without being marked as a target by well-bred women with marriage on their minds. Here, tossed up from the sea into the middle of nowhere, he was a man without a predetermined destiny.

He wasn't quite sure *who* he was, shorn of all the trappings that usually surrounded him, but he was willing to have a go at trying the situation out for size.

Especially in the company of a woman who looked the way this one did.

He felt a sudden tightness in his groin and had to stifle a need to groan aloud.

'Like I said,' he murmured, 'no one will have contacted the police to get a search party together just yet.' He commanded complete freedom of movement. He'd told his PA that he would be taking time out for a few days. He hadn't specified how many. She would have cancelled all immediate meetings and would have put nothing in place until told to do so. Likewise, his father would have no real idea when to expect him back. They didn't live in one another's pockets. As for the rest of the world...?

Who was there? He was an only child and a man who did as he pleased without reference to anyone else. He had never believed in the value of teamwork. The only person he had ever relied on was himself. It had served him well. Only now, he was struck by a certain peculiar uncertainty—a feeling that complete independence might not be quite what it was cracked up to be.

He shook his head impatiently.

'Walk me through your house,' he said gruffly, looking forward to immersing himself for a short while in a life that was far removed from his own.

'Only,' Cordelia returned, consumed with curiosity about the life he represented, 'if you tell me about your life in Italy.'

Luca relaxed. There was a lot he could tell her about his homeland. About the rolling splendour of

Tuscany, about the beauty of the Alps and the grandeur of the Apennines and the marvel of a climate, caught between the two, that was so perfect for growing the very best grapes, which produced the very best wine in the country. He could tell her about the villages surrounding his estate and the people who lived there, most of whom were employed in some capacity or other by his family and always had been.

Naturally, he would have to tailor all of it because there was even more he had no intention of telling her, starting with the truth of his identity and the position of power he held in the region.

She was leading the way out of the bedroom, onto the broad landing, vaguely pointing out the remaining bedrooms on the floor before heading down the wooden staircase into the body of the house.

Following in her wake, he was half paying attention but mostly looking at her and admiring the spring in her step, the way she half ran down the stairs. He was wondering what her hair would look like unrestrained. She had the longest hair he had ever seen.

They reached the black and white flagstone hall and she spun round to look at him, eyes bright and her expression open and trusting.

Luca blinked to dispel the weird ache that had kick-started inside him.

'I'll tell you everything you want to know about my country,' he said smoothly, 'on the condition that you tell me why you don't get out of here, or have I misinterpreted what you said earlier on?'

'You haven't and that's fair enough.' She smiled hesitantly and pulled the ponytail over one shoulder to distractedly play with it, twirling gold strands of hair between her fingers. She had so many questions she wanted to ask him that she didn't quite know where to begin.

And she could tell him so much about herself and why not? Her father wouldn't be back for another few hours. He was off fishing. And this man who had catapulted into her small, predictable world was so compelling.

Where was the harm in talking to him? It wasn't as though he were going to be around for much longer and it had been such a long time since she had talked, really talked, to a guy, to *anyone*. For ever. Her brother. That was how long it had been. So many years just plodding along, quietly doing what she had to do, without fuss, keeping her loneliness to herself.

Where was the harm in opening up, now, to this stranger...?

CHAPTER TWO

HE DIDN'T PHONE his father or his PA or anyone else for three days and when he did, it was to inform them that he had decided to take a slightly extended holiday. He'd be away for at least another week.

His PA had been a little startled but she was in her sixties, had worked for him for so long that she deserved a medal and had decided a decade ago that sorting out his emails and arranging his meetings was just a small part of her designated role.

'Take as much time out as you want, Luca,' she had soothed. 'You work too hard. You're thirty-four years old and you need to relax more or you'll have a heart attack before you know it. Stress. It kills. Those grapes will keep growing and the machinery will keep working until you decide to get back.'

His father had been largely indifferent. He'd handed over the reins of the sprawling family empire to his son a long time ago and had, since then, devoted his life to marrying and divorcing inappropriate women. Four at the last count although thankfully things had been quiet on that front for the past two years. Luca knew better than to expect that to last. He loved his father but he was far too aware of his failings to assume that a brief respite from unsuitable liaisons could herald anything more than the same old, same old.

And since then…

He looked at his watch. Then at the view spread out in front of him. From where he was sitting, waiting for her at the café on the waterfront, he had a splendid view of the harbour and just at the moment, with the sun shining, it was a picturesque sight. Blue water, the boats bobbing on the surface and people criss-crossing the road in front of him, taking their time getting out of the way should a beaten up car decide to drive past. It was a very far cry from the trendy seaside village where his house resided in a prestigious position on a hill overlooking a marina, which was dotted with expensive yachts and pleasure boats owned by the expensive people who flocked to the Michelin-starred restaurants and chic pubs and quaint tea rooms. The house was the last link to his mother, an expensive youthful present from way back when, when his father had slipped the engagement ring on her finger and led her to a house in the very place where she had grown up, so that she could maintain easy links with her friends and what little family she had left. His old man, even then, had done things in style.

That house summed up, for Luca, the way love and loss were so entwined, and, with everything going on in his life when he had decided to clear his desk and take time out, he had escaped back to it for just such a timely reminder. There was no such thing as love without loss.

He killed pointless musings dead.

As Cordelia had told him when she had shown him round the village two days previously, this was a working fishing village. There were occasional tourists in summer, in search of a more authentic Cornish experience, but largely the place was inhabited by locals, most of whom were involved in the fishing business in one way or the other.

As for Cordelia, Luca had discovered that she was a woman of many talents. Most of her time was spent helping her father run his small business. She did his books and, in summer, oversaw the rental of two of his boats further along the coast at one of the more popular seaside towns. She made sure that everything ticked along.

'Dad depends on me,' she had told him. 'I may not go out there on the trawler with him but I pretty much do everything else. Of course, if needs be, I'm more than capable of helping him at sea if one of the guys is off, but I'm better off staying here and working behind the scenes. He's hopeless when it comes to anything to do with filling in forms or paperwork and forget about computers.'

Luca saw her before she spotted him. She was glorious. Long limbs, arms swinging, her hair, as always, tied back. She radiated vitality and health and he marvelled that he had succeeded in keeping his hands to himself when he'd spent the last three days itching to reach out and touch her. His freedom might be on the brink of disappearing but, right now, he was still as single as the day was long.

But for once, he hadn't dared. There was an innocence about her that kept him at bay. For the first time in his life, he also had no idea how she would react if he made a pass at her. Slap him down? Kick him out of the house? Fling herself into his arms and beg for satisfaction? He had no idea and the uncertainty was paralysing.

He waved when she spotted him and she beamed back at him.

For a second, Luca felt a stab of guilt at the way he had played fast and loose with the truth. He'd talked a lot about his country but had been diplomatically light on detail. He knew that she'd somehow assumed that he'd been over on holiday, maybe chartered a boat for a day out, but the fact that he was hanging around had led her to assume that he was currently jobless and he hadn't disabused her of the notion. Why would he? He would soon be gone and this rare chance to be whoever he wanted to be was addictive.

'I've brought us a picnic.' Cordelia dumped a basket on the table and looked at him.

It was hot. A perfect summer day. This part of the world did perfect summer days like nowhere else. Bright blue sky, turquoise sea, clean smell of the ocean and the soft sound of the water slapping against the sides of the fishing boats.

She shielded her eyes from the glare and stared at him. With only the clothes on his back when she rescued him, he had had to buy a few more things and was wearing a pair of khaki shorts, some loafers and a white tee shirt. He looked magnificent. So exotic, so foreign...so much a vision of everything that was out of her orbit.

'And I've contributed in my own, small way.' He reached down to a cloth bag on the ground and when she looked inside, she saw two bottles of champagne.

'Wow.'

'If you're going to do something, then you don't do it in half measures.'

'But champagne... It must have cost a fortune.'

'I won't worry about the price tag if you don't.'

'I like that,' she confided as they began heading out towards where her boat was anchored just off the jetty.

'What?'

'The fact that you're so carefree.' She slid her eyes across to him and drank in the lean beauty of his face. His hair was longer than when she'd brought him back to the house, curling at the nape of his neck.

'I don't think anyone has ever described me as carefree before,' Luca commented with complete honesty. 'Frankly, it's not a description I would ever have used for myself.'

'Wouldn't you? Why not?' She glanced at him, smiling, then began the business of getting the boat ready for them while he watched and admired her quiet efficiency, doing something she had probably done a million times before. It was compulsive viewing. She was wearing some cut-off jeans and a striped tee shirt. He could just about make out the heavy swing of her breasts as she expertly loosened the boat from its mooring, bringing it into position for them. She had braided her hair into one long plait that fell down the centre of her spine like rope.

'You're here,' she pointed out, steadying the boat and then half jumping on board without really looking where she put her feet because the manoeuvre was so familiar. 'You're not rushing off to do anything. You know how to slow down. So many people don't, although I guess if you're going to slow down, then this is the perfect place to do it and the perfect time, given what you went through.'

Cordelia watched as he hit the deck as confidently as she had. When he suggested he sail the boat, she found herself instantly agreeing because something inside her trusted his expertise, which was contrary to everything she had been brought up to believe.

'Everyone thinks they know what to do when it comes to boats,' her father had told both her and her brother when they were young. 'Don't trust anyone with a throttle, a rudder, a tiller or an engine unless they can produce a captain's licence. It's easy to get out of your depth when it comes to handling a boat, and out at sea, that could be fatal. I'll make sure the pair of you know exactly what to do when you get on a boat. If anyone gets on with you and asks for a go, tell them to get lost.'

She gave directions, sat back and tilted her face up to the sun.

'Do you ever slow down?' Luca murmured, obeying directions, enjoying the speed of the boat as it sliced through the water to the hidden bay she had told him about, enjoying even more the feel of her next to him, her body warmed from the sun, the hairs on her hands white-blonde in the sun.

'Only when I do this,' she replied, eyes still closed. 'Or when I go swimming. I slow right down when I go swimming. Especially if I go swimming at night.'

'At night...and you don't get scared?'

'Of what? I know everything there is to know about the tides around here. I'd never swim if there was a hint of a current, but if the water's calm, then there's something about being in it when it's dark. I can think.'

They'd arrived at the bay. It was deserted and protected by dense shrubbery and tangled trees. The sand was very white and, when they stepped out onto it, already warm from the sun.

'What do you think about?'

Cordelia looked at him and couldn't look away. She'd thought long and hard about what to tell him about herself and, in the end, had said very little. She was ever so slightly in awe of him. He was like a bright, tropical bird of paradise, blown in on the winds, and every time she had felt that urge to confide, she had been overcome by a surge of shyness.

'This and that.' She shrugged and broke eye contact to set up a little picnic area in the shade of one of the overhanging trees. When she turned round to look at him, he had divested himself of his tee shirt and was staring out at the horizon with his back to her.

Her heart sped up. He was a few inches taller than her and perfectly proportioned. Broad-shouldered, narrow-waisted, lean-hipped. He'd shoved his hands into the pockets of his shorts. He'd asked her what she'd been thinking but now she wished she could see into his head, find out what *he* was thinking. His life in Italy sounded idyllic. 'Vineyards,' he had told her, waving aside more in-depth questioning, as though working on a vineyard was something she couldn't possibly find that interesting.

'Grapes...' he had shrugged, when she breathlessly asked for details '...that's pretty much all there is to say on the subject of vineyards. Grapes. You either eat them or you turn them into wine. I'm involved in the latter option.'

She was still shamelessly gawping when he spun round to look at her and she reddened.

'Tell me you're not going to spend the day in jeans and a tee shirt,' he encouraged with a grin. 'Did you bring a swimsuit or do you have plans on skinny dipping?'

Cordelia made a strangled sound under her breath and hastily got rid of her jeans and tee shirt to reveal a sensible black whole piece. Skinny dipping? The thought alone brought her out in a cold sweat.

'Ah, swimming costume. Good. It would be a sin not to try the water on a day like this.' Luca had never seen anyone under the age of eighty in a swimsuit as sensible as the one she was wearing and yet, conversely, had never been so tempted to touch. Her legs were long and shapely, the lines of her body strong and athletic, her skin pale gold.

He averted his eyes but there was a steady pulsing in his groin that was going to prove embarrassing if he carried on giving free rein to his imagination.

Cold water had never looked so inviting. He

stepped out of the khakis, down to the swimming trunks he had bought a couple of days earlier.

'Think I need a swim,' he gritted, baring his teeth in something he hoped would resemble a relaxed smile. 'So hot.' He waded straight into the ice-cold water. Felt good. Anything to douse the rise in his body temperature when he had looked at her.

He didn't look back for five minutes and when he did, it was to find that she was striking out in his direction, in long, fluid strokes that ate up the distance between them.

She hadn't been lying when she'd told him that she could swim like a fish. She could. And out here, in the ocean where blue yielded to black because it was so much deeper, she was in her natural element. He could see that as soon as she had caught up with him. There was real pleasure on her face and she was smiling. All the hesitancy and shyness that seemed part and parcel of her personality had disappeared. She looked as though she had barely broken a sweat swimming out to him.

'You're a strong swimmer,' she told him, treading water.

'You're surprised because you thought I was a wimp who could barely man a boat and had to rely on being rescued by a damsel in shining armour because of his own stupidity?'

'Something like that.'

Luca burst out laughing and cast appreciative eyes

over her face. She truly had the most amazing eyes, he thought. A shade somewhere between navy blue and bright turquoise with a hint of green and, for a blonde, her lashes were lush and dark.

'Race you back?' Cordelia backed away in the water. The way he was looking at her...she'd caught that expression before, a fleeting glimpse of something heated and *dangerous*, but she had told herself that it was her imagination playing tricks on her. She lacked the sophistication to interpret those kinds of games and she didn't trust herself to even try. It was a lot easier to pretend there was nothing there, that any wayward expression she might have glimpsed in him was all in her mind. Why would a man like Luca look at a woman like her? He was so beautiful, so exotic, so compelling while she...was a country girl who worked her fingers to the bone in the fishing business. Vineyard versus fishing. Even if all he did was pick grapes and do whatever people did to grapes when they were picked, it was still impossibly glamorous as far as she was concerned.

She didn't wait for his response. She began swimming and all the thoughts left her head as she felt the cold water sluice against her body and the exertion of the swim heating her up until the sea was warm against her skin.

He kept pace and then increased it so that he hit the shoreline before she did.

She was laughing when she emerged from the

water. Her hair was still in the braid but she tugged the elastic band off and rifled her fingers through its length so that it spread over her shoulders and down her back, reaching all the way to her waist.

Luca felt as though he'd been punched in the gut and he was breathing heavily as he turned away to open the bottle of champagne. Hell, she might be fine with this scenario but he was in desperate need of a drink. He only wished he'd thought to bring something a little stronger. A bottle of whisky would have done the trick. Instead, he popped the cork on the champagne, which was still cold thanks to the sleeve into which it had been put, and he extended one of the two plastic glasses to her.

'Are there rules about drinking and sailing?' he asked, sitting on a rock while she tidily spread an oversized rug on the sand.

'I've brought lots of water.' She smiled and sipped some champagne. 'And lots of food. That should take care of the alcohol.'

'If it doesn't, we could always spend the night on the beach.' Their eyes tangled and he slanted a smile at her. 'I guess living here, that's something you must have done a million times…?'

Luca knew that he was shamelessly fishing for information but he wanted to find out more about her, dig a bit deeper, which was something he was seldom inclined to do when it came to the opposite sex. He'd long discovered that the women he dated were all largely gifted in the art of talking about themselves. There was almost no need to ask questions.

'Not once,' Cordelia murmured thoughtfully. 'Although there are loads of bays and coves around here and, yes, there were always parties during the summer holidays.'

'But you didn't go to them.'

She swallowed some more champagne and grimaced. 'When I was twelve, one of my friends had a birthday party on a cove not far from this one. Of course, adults were there. Since then, I've only ever sailed to one of these coves on my own.'

'No reckless teenage parties with contraband alcohol and furious parents hunting down their wayward offspring to drag them back home?'

'Not for me.'

'Why not?'

'Because…' The sun was beating down but the rug was under the shade of a tree and there was just enough of a balmy breeze to make her feel sleepy. He'd left the rock at some point and was on the rug with her, sitting up, but then he lay flat, staring up at the cloudless blue sky, and she followed suit. 'Because my father was very protective. My mother died when I was young. I told you that, but after she died, Dad, somehow, developed a crazy fear that if I ventured too far, something bad would happen. Of course, I didn't notice it at all when I was young, but the older I got…the more I realised that I didn't have the same freedoms as loads of kids my age. But then, my brother died and everything got…so much more difficult.' She paused and gathered herself.

'You had a brother? I had no idea.'

'Why would you? Dad never talks about Alex. In fact, when he died, Dad made sure that all the framed photos of him were taken down. Alex was my twin.'

She was surprised and then moved when she felt Luca link his fingers through hers. Her mind was engaged in the past, but she still felt a jolt of electricity run through her body. The warmth of his fingers was so good, so reassuring and it was the first physical contact they had shared since she looked after him. Excitement leaped inside her but she told herself that this was just the normal gesture of someone empathising with what she had just said. The equivalent of a hug. Hugs weren't sexual. A brotherly hug from a friend didn't end up in a steamy kiss. But she still liked the touch of those fingers…and the thought of a steamy kiss was…well…in her head before she could take defensive measures to keep it out.

'Your twin!'

He levered himself into a half-sitting position and leaned over her, to stare at her with startled, concerned eyes.

Cordelia dealt with that by closing her eyes. His fingers were still linked with hers and having him so close to her, close enough to feel his warm breath on her cheek, was too much to handle.

'Everything changed after Alex died,' Cordelia said. 'I'd planned on going to university, even though I knew that Dad would have to resist phoning twice a day to make sure I was all right. I think he always felt, deep down, that he should have been able to protect my mum, that he should have been there with her when she went to London, then she wouldn't have been hit by that car and everything would have been all right. If he couldn't protect Mum, then he would devote his life to protecting me. But going to university?' She sighed. 'I'd worked out that it was just something I had to do. Alex was destined to help Dad in the fishing business and eventually take it over. It was all he'd ever wanted to do whereas I...'

'Whereas you...?'

'I had dreams of leaving here, seeing what was out there. It would have been the right thing to do for me and for my dad. Instead, those dreams died with Alex. I had no choice but to step into his shoes. Don't get me wrong, it's not a bad life, but there's a big world out there and I've resigned myself to the fact that I'll never get to see it.'

She opened her eyes to find that he was still staring down at her and she smiled.

'I'm not about to start weeping and wailing on you,' she said.

'I have no objection to a weeping and wailing woman,' Luca lied. He could have expanded. He could have told her that weeping and wailing set his teeth on edge. He'd had his fill of watching the antics of his father's ex-wives, the emotional dramas played out for public consumption when the marriages began to unravel. He could remember one memorable occasion when one of his father's birthday celebrations had descended into full-blown farce when an inebriated wife number three had decided to spill the beans on everything she hated about men, and about his father in particular. So weeping and wailing? No chance.

'Liar.' But the smile was more heartfelt this time. 'Men hate women crying on them.'

'You speak from experience? Some guy turn on you because you cried?'

'No!' She couldn't resist any longer and she reached out and stroked the side of his face and noticed that her fingers were trembling. It was only a stroke, but it felt as daring as if she'd done a striptease. Her nipples were pinched into tight, sensitive buds and heat had bloomed between her thighs.

The warm sun, the champagne, the sharing of these confidences…and this enigmatic stranger. The mix was heady and combustible.

'No guys?' He held still her hand and then opened it and, eyes still on her, he kissed her palm, then licked it, the delicate trace of his tongue on her skin.

She sighed and trembled, caught between an urge to pull back because this was dangerous territory and a need to go further because she'd never done a dangerous thing in her entire life and the temptation was overpowering.

She felt as if she'd spent so long looking through a pane of glass at a world filled with exciting possibilities that the chance to go past that glass and actually have a taste of that excitement was too much to resist.

She shifted, her breathing quickening, invitation playing on her parted lips.

'I've told you all about myself,' she whispered shakily. 'It's your turn to tell me all about yourself.'

'I've done nothing but tell you about myself for the past few days…' *How to redefine the truth?* That was the thought that ran through Luca's head, but he swept aside that momentary discomfort.

'I guess the work is seasonal, which is why you can afford to take time off and stay here…'

When are you going to go?

She found that the prospect of him leaving made her feel weirdly hollow inside.

'There are more optimum months for harvesting the grapes…that's true…'

'And what do you do when you're not picking them? Do you travel? Visit family? Who do you live with in Italy?'

'That's a lot of questions, *tesoro*…'

'I'm curious about you. For so many reasons, I'm stuck here. You can't blame me for asking questions.' She looked at him wistfully, imagining his world, which would be so different from hers. A world without obligations and responsibilities, where work was something that could be picked up and dropped on a whim. Maybe he did other, odd jobs, aside from the grape picking, although she doubted it because his knowledge of the wine industry was so detailed. He obviously loved what he did.

'No, I can't,' Luca told her honestly. 'But guilt is no way to lead your life, *cara*. You're too young to think that you're stuck somewhere without hope of escape, looking at places on a map and assuming you'll never get to visit any of them.'

'You've met my father. You've seen for yourself that I can't just waltz off in the sunset...'

Luca shrugged. Yes, he had met Clive Ramsey, a weathered man in his sixties whose life revolved around his daughter and the sea. He'd lost his wife and he'd never really moved on. Just another example of what a waste of time love was. It got its hooks into you and from that point on, you were on a road to nowhere. Luca struggled to think of a single example of all that starry-eyed, fairy-tale rubbish soppy movies promoted.

In fairness, Clive hadn't been around much. The fishing season was at its height and he was gone most days and many nights, trawling for crab and lobster, leaving the running of the house and his business to the daughter he clearly couldn't do without. Luca was sure things would have been different had her brother lived, but now, as she'd told him, she'd had no choice but to step up to the plate.

He suddenly had an overwhelming urge to take her away and show her all those faraway sights she had only ever dreamed about.

'We're talking too much,' he murmured, bringing things back down to familiar terrain. 'Let's just enjoy being here.'

Cordelia smiled, heart swelling with excitement. There was nothing she yearned for more than to enjoy the moment for what it was. She wanted so much for him to touch her, really touch her, but her lack of experience was crippling.

He was attracted to her. She knew he was, unbelievable as it was. That was a start in the right direction.

'No one ever comes to this cove,' she confided nervously. 'At least not during the day...'

'Shame. It's exquisite.'

'It's because you need a boat to get here. It's inaccessible from land. Not that many people have boats that they can just take out for the fun of it.'

'Lucky you.'

'I feel it. Right now. Lucky, I mean...' she said breathlessly. She shifted onto her side and shuffled a bit closer in what she hoped were movements barely visible to the naked eye.

She fought down a wave of nervous nausea and

ran her hands softly over his stomach, enjoying the feel of muscled strength under her fingers.

She saw the look of astonishment in his eyes and was tempted to pull her hand away, but she didn't because something inside her knew that if she didn't seize this moment, it would never be there for the taking again.

'Cordelia…' Luca said in a roughened undertone, shifting but not doing what he knew he should be doing, namely removing himself from temptation. He hadn't been able to resist touching that satiny smooth skin but alarm bells in his head were louder than the church bells in his local village.

'I really like you…' she admitted, blushing furiously but maintaining eye contact.

Luca groaned and clenched his jaw hard. He was rock hard. If he glanced down, he knew that he wouldn't be able to miss the sizeable bulge underneath the still slightly damp trunks. Nor would she. If she'd been more brazen, it would have been easy to pull away, however attractive he found her, but her innocence, the courage to say what she had, which he could tell was costing her dear, her damned *back story*, was lethally persuasive.

She reached out for his hand and he felt the tremor in her fingers. He heard himself say something softly under his breath when she placed his hand on her breast and then, shockingly, reached to stroke his thigh.

Not courageous enough to touch what clearly

needed touching, but it didn't matter because what she was doing was sending his body into explosive overdrive. Those little circular motions with her finger, gentle and delicate. They made him wonder what it would feel like to have her tongue there, and that elicited another guttural groan of desire.

'This…' He struggled to sound normal. 'Not a good idea…'

She immediately removed her hand. 'I was wrong. You don't fancy me. I understand.'

Luca couldn't answer. Instead, he grasped her hand and returned it to his thigh.

'I've never wanted any woman more in my life,' he confessed shakily. 'But…'

'But I guess you're more accustomed to sexy, dark-haired Italian women…'

'You need to look in the mirror a little more often, *la mia bellezza.*'

He drew her close, pressed her against him while the sun poured down like honey and the impossibly blue sea stifled all the perfectly sound thoughts in his head, hypnotising him into wanting one thing and one thing only. Her.

By way of response, Cordelia nuzzled his neck and then tentatively covered his thigh with her own. She could feel his hard erection pulsing against her belly and she desperately wanted to put her hand over it, feel it moving, but when she actually thought of doing that, she felt faint.

She had zero experience when it came to men. At least, none of her fumbling adventures, such as they'd been, were worth writing home about.

She hadn't avoided sex. She'd never had any puritanical ideals to turn it into some kind of prize to be handed to the right guy. No, as luck would have it, she'd just had the one semi-serious boyfriend and they hadn't ended up in bed. Now she knew why. She hadn't been turned on. She hadn't had the foggiest idea what being turned on *was all about*. Because *this* was what it felt like to be turned on. *This* was what had been missing from the equation.

This and so many other things.

This was excitement. Heart-stopping, pulse-racing, nerve-jangling excitement and if he wanted her, then she couldn't begin to describe just how much *she* wanted *him*.

CHAPTER THREE

SHE FELL BACK compliantly when he pushed her gently so that he could lever himself up to stare down at her. His breathing was a heavy rasp and his eyes were dark with passion, unfocused, as though he had been transported to another world.

He ran his hand along her side and then up along her ribcage. The almost dry swimsuit was an irritant, a scratchy barrier between them that Cordelia wanted to yank off but, again, her lack of experience was paralysing. She didn't have the confidence to take the reins and she wondered whether that lack of confidence and experience would be a turn-off for him.

He was so...*sexy*. So dark, so exotic, so unbelievably, sinfully *compelling*. You didn't have to let your imagination wander too far to realise that he wouldn't have lived a life deprived of adoring women and it wasn't just about his looks. Over the past few days, she had seen the three-dimensional man who had not been in evidence when he'd been in and out of sleep for the first couple of days after she had rescued him.

He was dry, witty, funny and a brilliant listener. He had painted such vivid images in her head of the bright Italian sun streaming down on acre upon acre of carefully cultivated vineyards. He could describe the colour and texture of the fat, juicy grapes with the detail of a poet and his adventures...the places he'd visited! Cordelia could only assume that he used the pay he made working in the wine industry to travel the world when the harvesting season came to an end.

In every way, shape and form his life was a window to a faraway world she could only dream of.

And here he was, with her, and the need to have this man and enjoy this moment was overpowering.

She tentatively drew his hand to her breast and felt him shudder against her.

When he made a half-hearted motion to remove it, she held it fast and was filled with a sense of reckless daring.

'Cordelia,' he groaned under his breath. 'Like I said...this isn't a good idea...'

'Why? If you fancy me and I fancy you, why isn't it a good idea?'

'A million reasons,' he murmured, but he was touching her, massaging the full weight of her breast in his big hand and then slipping a finger under the strap of the swimsuit so that he could slowly draw it down.

Her eyelids fluttered shut and she sighed and then arched up as the swimsuit was pulled down. She twisted and moaned and linked her fingers behind his head and drew him lower. She could feel the conflict inside him but she knew that temptation was stronger than the voice of reason. Inexperienced she might be, but she *knew* that with unerring, feminine certainty. He wanted her and he couldn't help himself and that filled her with a sense of heady power.

Everything about this man was an eye-opener and she was loving it.

His mouth circled her nipple and he flicked his tongue over the stiffened bud and began teasing it into such fierce arousal that a hum of sensation began between her thighs, growing in intensity until she was rubbing her legs together in an attempt to control it.

She was desperate for his hand to be there and, as if reading her mind, he cupped her between her legs. When she wriggled against the palm of his hand, he obligingly and gently pressed down.

Her body was behaving in all sorts of wild and wonderful ways.

Not knowing what she was supposed to do with *him*, she slid her hand over his muscled thigh and shuddered.

'All in good time.' Luca's voice was husky and only just the right side of controlled.

He nuzzled her breast and then moved to the other and laved it with his tongue.

It was unbearable. She parted her legs and trembled when he immediately slid his hand under the stretchy Lycra of the swimsuit, distorting it as he began to rub her there.

He removed his hand and then began easing the swimsuit off her, all the while licking her nipple and suckling on her breast. She couldn't think straight. Couldn't think *at all*.

She just wanted him on her and in her and she wanted it in a hurry.

Her hands scrabbled at his swimming trunks.

Luca stilled. There was enough common sense still left in him to realise that this was not in the plan. Yes, he'd looked at her and discovered that his libido could reach heights he could never have anticipated, but he'd fast worked out that that was only partially to do with the fact that she was attractive.

Maybe more than *just attractive*.

He'd worked out that it was due to a combination of things, not least the fact that he was away from normality, away from the trappings of power and wealth that had always defined him and away from the people who lived in that rarefied world. He was a free man here and so everything was heightened, including the mystifying power of his attraction to the woman lying in this slice of empty paradise.

So many responsibilities awaited his return that freedom had never tasted sweeter.

Was it, therefore, so surprising that he could barely string two coherent thoughts together when he was around the woman?

He'd replaced his computer on day four when he'd headed out to get himself a handful of new clothes to replace the ones he had borrowed from her father. He'd hit the nearest town, headed for an Internet café and rebooted his working life, but even the pressing emails and endless reports and the lucrative deals with companies abroad awaiting his attention couldn't quite manage to distract him from whatever spell had been weaved on him.

Luca was loving it all. Accustomed as he was to a life of staggering control and predictability, he was thoroughly enjoying the sensation of letting himself go.

Which didn't mean that he'd turned into the village idiot! He always used protection but right now, right here...

For the first time in his life, the thrill of the gamble was greater than the pull of common sense. He knew what he should do and what he shouldn't but there was a weakness inside him, driving him on to take a chance, *just this once*.

She was still naked and so, so beautiful and he still had an erection as hard as a rod of steel.

He felt the slickness between her legs because he just couldn't *not* go there.

'Okay.'

'You're a siren.' His groan was unsteady. 'I can picture you sitting on a rock out there, calling to sailors. They wouldn't stand a chance.'

He levered himself down, trailing his tongue along her body and tasting the salt from the sea. Her breasts and stomach were paler, emphasising the rich pink of her nipples, each tipped with stiffened buds the colour of claret. He played briefly with one nipple, teasing it between two fingers, but then he moved to circle her slender waist with his hands. He stroked her hips with the pads of his thumbs, then he moved even lower to gently peel apart the groove between her thighs that sheathed the pulsing of her clitoris.

He licked it, tasted her honeyed sweetness and felt himself swell even more at her little whimpers and soft, startled moans and the way she moved against his mouth, bumping up and down and wriggling, keeping his head in place because her fingers were curled into his over-long hair, and panting.

'Please…' she breathed and that simple plea scattered that well-intentioned voice of reason to the four winds.

He couldn't resist.

Not when she was like this, her slender legs spread apart, open to him like a flower, inviting him to come inside. Reason, logic, forward-thinking... His brain shut down, leaving him at the mercy of sensation.

Shaking with desire, Luca stood up to rid himself of his swimming trunks, pausing only to smile at the rapt attention on her face.

Cordelia smiled back. Was it an alluring, siren-like smile, or a nervous I've-never-done-this-before smile?

She desperately hoped that he would think the former. She wanted him so badly.

'You're right,' she whispered with gut-wrenching disappointment because this felt like a do-or-die situation. They would not relive this opportunity, not when they were back in the house and she was busy once again with the accounts and phone calls and making sure everything was okay with the house and the various things that needed to be done in it.

'This is crazy.' She blushed and looked away and felt the gentle touch of his finger under her chin.

'Everyone needs a little crazy now and again. Don't talk. I can't talk. I just...want you...'

Her whole body was trembling. So was his. He'd never felt anything like it before. He'd never felt this *need* before. It was like being in the grip of a tornado.

He came inside her in one deep, satisfying thrust. Her tightness encased him perfectly and he groaned and moved, deeper, feeling his shaft sinking into her wetness.

The sensation was so intense he wanted to pass out. There was no artistry in this lovemaking. It was frantic, driving and mind-blowing. She bucked underneath him, arching and stiffening and her short nails dug into his back. He came fast and hard. He could feel the swell and release as he pumped into her, sucking the wild energy out of him and leaving him breathing hard and deeply, shockingly sated.

'Oh, God,' he groaned. He lay flat on his back and shielded his eyes for a few seconds from the glare of the sun. Breathing normally was still a problem as his body came down from its high. 'I've never been like that before.' It was a struggle to think. 'Was it... okay for you?'

'More than okay,' Cordelia whispered under her breath and he turned onto his side to look at her. She angled her body so that they were facing one another.

It was so beautifully warm and the sound of the water lapping against the sand was hypnotic.

'If I could bottle this,' she confessed with honesty, 'then I would.' She stroked his cheek and edged closer to kiss his chin. Her whole body was still thrumming from where he had entered her. She'd felt a twinge of discomfort but her body had been ripe and ready for his entry and the bigness of him inside her, the way he'd moved, had taken her to places she'd never dreamed existed. She'd felt the surge of his orgasm meshing with her own. Their bodies had been as one, united. She couldn't wait to touch him again, to make love again.

How could they not when it had felt so good?

There were no alarm bells ringing in her head. She was on cloud nine and it was only when their eyes met that she wondered whether too much honesty about how much she'd enjoyed what had just happened between them might not be such a great idea.

'Cordelia,' Luca murmured, clasping her hand between his and pensively stroking her chin with his thumb. He sighed. 'That was better than great.'

She beamed.

'You have a smile that could light up a room,' he said, distractedly.

'Thank you. I don't think anyone's ever said that to me before.'

'Maybe because there aren't sufficient eligible men around here to notice it. But trust me, you have.' He looked at her in silence for a few seconds. 'What we did...we shouldn't have done,' he said bluntly, because beating round the bush had never been his thing. 'I don't know what happened. Things got out of hand. I...wanted you, wanted to feel myself in you. I was in the grip of...something bigger than common sense. I still don't understand... It's unheard of, if I'm being honest.' He shook his head, genuinely bewildered. 'I'm usually in control of…everything. I don't get it.'

'Of everything?' Cordelia smiled, because what he was saying was music to her ears. 'Is that possible?'

'God, yes. I certainly have never lost control when it comes to sex, but I did this time and for that I apologise.'

'Luca…don't apologise. I…' *I absolutely adored it, loved it, was blown away by it…* 'I really enjoyed what we did.'

She'd never thought about what sex might *feel* like. She'd vaguely assumed that it was something that would happen sooner or later, when she found someone she actually wanted to date, someone she could envisage sharing her life with. That such a person hadn't come along yet had not filled her with any sense of disappointment. Frankly, looking around at the nearby talent, she'd felt relieved that marriage and everything it entailed wasn't high on her agenda because the choice of candidates for the post of potential life partner was lamentably non-existent.

Dreaming of the great, big world out there was a lot more fun.

And now…the great, big world had landed on her doorstep!

'It's not just about losing control,' Luca said roughly. 'I'm no good for you.'

'What are you talking about?'

'That was good sex.' He decided that bringing it down to basics would kick the conversation off to a good start, put things in perspective for her. 'Better than good,' he amended. He thought back to the urgings that had prompted him to throw caution to the winds and taste, just for one wild moment, what it felt like to be inside her. *Better than good* didn't come close to an adequate description. She'd been so unbelievably, fantastically tight around him. He frowned and focused.

'But I need to remind you that this isn't the start of…any kind of relationship. I'm not one of the local lads who's going to come knocking on your father's door to take you out on a date.'

'I know that.' She broke eye contact. The pulse in her neck was racing madly, and for some reason what he'd just said stung. She sat up abruptly and drew her knees up to her chin and stared out to sea. It was empty. No passing boats. No ship on the horizon. Nothing to make you think that you were anywhere but alone on an island in the middle of the ocean. When she glanced over her shoulder to him, it was to find him looking at her with pensive, brooding intensity.

It was a ridiculous conversation to have when they were both naked, she thought with a spurt of anger.

She felt suddenly vulnerable even though, lying there, he obviously couldn't give a hoot whether he was clothed or not. She glanced down and immediately diverted her eyes. Erect or not, he was ridiculously impressive.

She felt her body jerk into uninvited reaction and clicked her tongue with annoyance because she'd just been given the brush-off, in so many words, and the last thing she should be doing by way of response was getting worked up all over again.

'Do you?'

Cordelia gritted her teeth and ignored him completely as she sprang to her feet and hastily donned the swimsuit that had been shed with such enthusiasm less than an hour earlier.

Much better.

'Of course.' Her voice was a lot more normal when she looked at him now, as were her pulse rate and the general state of her nervous system.

'If you hadn't ended up half drowning...' she said.

'Don't remind me. Men have fragile egos when it comes to that kind of thing.'

'We would never have met. But here you are and I don't think, for a second, that this is the start of any kind of relationship. I'm not on the lookout for a relationship! But I don't get to adventure much and this is *fun*.'

'Good. So we understand one another.'

'Does every woman you happen to sleep with need a warning just in case they start thinking that you're interested in a long-term, full-time relationship?' She folded her arms and stared at him. He raised his eyebrows, amused, and she blushed scarlet when she had visible proof that he was getting aroused once again.

He idly took himself in his hand while he continued to look at her, and she reddened further.

He took his time standing up but even then he didn't put on the discarded swimming trunks, choosing instead to saunter down to the water, whereupon he turned to look at her.

'Another swim? Or food?'

Cordelia frowned. She was fairly certain that this was a serious conversation that should be afforded a suitable amount of gravitas. Instead, that crooked half-smile of his held just the hint of an invitation, and she found herself walking towards him, pulled in his direction by invisible strings.

She pictured him sitting on that rug in all his glory, tucking into the sandwiches she had made and wearing nothing but his birthday suit, and she strode into the water.

'Well?' She turned to him and folded her arms. 'Do you always think that you have to warn women off in case they start expecting more than you want to give?'

'More than I'm capable of giving,' Luca surprised himself by saying.

'What do you mean? What are you talking about?'

'I'm talking about me, Cordelia. Me, women and my experiences with them.' He turned away and began swimming out, his strokes long and clean, and she followed until they were both out in the deep blue ocean, their bodies adjusted to the cold, cold water, which felt good in the burning heat of the midday sun.

She flipped over onto her back and felt the sun pouring down over her. When she glanced across it was to find that he had done the same.

For one fleeting second she questioned what she had got herself into. This wasn't the boy next door. This wasn't one of the local lads who drank at the same pub every weekend and followed their dad into the same family business. Those were the boys she knew and was accustomed to.

This guy was all dark and dangerous and out of her league and if he was also funny and sharp and challenging, she knew that she should still never forget that there was a lot more to him than that.

Maybe that was part and parcel of the tingle that rippled through her as she feasted her eyes on his averted profile.

She'd never had a single experience with any man. He'd been her first.

He'd obviously had so many experiences with women that he had built up a portfolio on their behaviour patterns and expectations when it came to relationships.

Mingled with simmering excitement, a certain amount of unease nudged its way through but she blithely shoved that aside because, as he'd just reminded her, he was just passing through. People who were passing through didn't cause problems. It was the ones who stuck around and made a nuisance of themselves you had to be wary of.

'You sound like an old man,' she half joked.

'There are times I feel like one,' Luca said heavily.

'Don't you believe in love?'

'Strangely, I don't believe anyone's ever asked me that question directly before.' He sounded surprised. 'But now that you've asked, I don't. I don't believe in love, I don't believe in the fairy tales people insist on telling that there's such a thing as a happy-ever-after. You're young, *mi tesoro*, which is why I felt that I should warn you off me.'

'And like I've told you, there's no need. Why don't you? Believe in love and marriage, I mean?' She thought of herself in a white dress floating down the aisle on her father's arm, to meet the man of her dreams. Instantly, a few pedestrian details jarred the dreamy image. Firstly the thought of herself in a dress, which was an item of clothing she didn't possess, and secondly the thought of what this man of her dreams would look like.

Tall, dark and handsome.

Like the one lying next to her floating on the gently rolling water.

But, she hurriedly amended in her head, clearly *not* the one next to her. Maybe one similar.

'Oh, but I do believe in marriage,' Luca said wryly. He thought of Isabella, waiting for him back in Italy, and a sharp tug of guilt drove into him with the force of a serrated knife cutting through skin. There was nothing to feel guilty about. He knew that. At least, the cold, logical side of his brain knew that. He was on the same page as the woman floating alongside him so what if, besides the fact that he wouldn't be sticking around, another very valid reason for him being the least suitable man on the planet for her lay in the fact that he was practically engaged to someone? Did that matter? No, of course it didn't because a relationship wasn't on the table and he'd been brutally honest in making that clear.

Aside from which…he was fond of Isabella and she was perfect for him because she would never ask for what he couldn't give. They would marry and two great families would unite and, of course, they would be careful about their outside interests because, under the guise of marriage, they would be as brother and sister. She and her girlfriend, Ella, would carry on seeing one another and he…he would discreetly do what any red-blooded man would have to do to satisfy his libido. For a man who did not believe or trust in love, it would be the ideal marriage.

And yet…

Suddenly restless, he began swimming back to shore, making sure that Cordelia was following him and then slinging his arm around her shoulders as they stepped out of the water. He retrieved the swimming trunks and put them on.

'You just haven't found the right woman? Is that it?' Cordelia returned to the conversation as she began unpacking the picnic, carefully putting the contents of Tupperware containers on the rug and not looking directly at him.

'There's no such thing as the *right* woman. There is, however, such a thing as a *suitable* woman. I want to have a family as much as the next person,' he confided with utmost honesty. 'I also want to have a successful marriage and, as far as I'm concerned, those two things are perfectly possible provided there are no unreasonable expectations on either side.' He paused and Isabella flashed into his head once again. For all her sexual proclivities, they would produce the requisite heir. A discreet consultant would easily facilitate that. The signatures weren't exactly on the paper yet, but they would be by the time he returned to Italy.

The business of love would never complicate matters. Luca wondered whether that was why he had returned to Cornwall, to remind himself of what he already knew. Love had destroyed his father and Cornwall was a symbol of that love. You could almost say that that was where the story began.

'I don't suppose that's exactly your cup of tea, is it?' He looked at her, appreciating, yet again, the white-blonde tangle of her hair flowing down her back and over her shoulders…the healthy gold of her skin, so much darker than where the sun didn't touch…the intense violet of her eyes…the athleticism of her strong body. Jesus, was he hardening *again*?

'Not at all,' Cordelia admitted lightly. She passed him a chunky ham and cheese sandwich on a paper plate and sat back on her haunches to look at him for a few seconds. The glare was sharp and she was squinting into the sun. 'Not many women would accept that sort of situation.'

'You'd be surprised,' Luca murmured in response. It felt as if he'd already said too much. Sitting here, talking about this touchy-feely stuff…made him vaguely uneasy. Something about her lulled him into feeling just so damned *comfortable*. 'Nice sandwich.' He changed the subject, steering firmly away from dangerous ground. 'Generous.'

Cordelia burst out laughing at his expression. 'I've spent too many years making sandwiches for my dad and some of the other fishermen to switch from sandwiches like these to delicate little cucumber ones.' She sobered up and settled into a more comfortable position. 'Why don't you believe in love? What happened?'

Luca looked at her. Her expression was open and quizzical. No agenda there. She was so much a part of this wild, beautiful, Cornish slice of land and yet as trapped in it as he was trapped in his own privileged, rarefied world, if only she knew.

He experienced a moment of such perfect *oneness* that he had to clear his throat and make a conscious effort to gather himself.

'I don't...' *Don't talk about my private life to anyone, ever.* 'I don't know what happened, but I've figured out over the years that my father's disastrous personal life had something to do with it.' He paused. There was an odd, swooping sensation in the pit of his stomach that he had never experienced before. She was quietly working her way through her sandwich and thoroughly enjoying it. He'd brought champagne but he figured she would be the sort of girl who wouldn't mind a pint now and again. He had an insane desire to introduce her to his wines, watch her taste the soft subtleties on her palate and, again, he had to shake himself back into the moment and remember, *with relief*, that in the blink of an eye he would walk away, back to reality, never to see her again.

'I know how that feels.' She smiled ruefully, prompting him to do the unthinkable and continue.

'My mother died when I was young.' His smile matched hers. 'We may have more in common than you think because her death blew a hole in my father's life and he was never the same since. Unlike your father, though, he didn't emotionally retreat from the world and he certainly didn't become overprotective of me. The opposite. My father has made a career out of trying to find a substitute for what he lost. Never succeeded.'

'Do you have siblings?'

'No. There's just me.'

No twin, as you had, to share the loneliness and grief, just a father walking away as he tried to carve a life of his own to fill his own void, leaving his only son to work things out for himself.

'Holding the fort, so to speak.' He thought of those vast acres of vineyards and the incomparable wealth, growing daily under his studious, watchful eye. Her idea of the fort in question would bear no resemblance to reality, that was for sure.

'Working to keep things ticking over. Like me.' She had a vision of him, so strong, labouring under the sun, watching out for his father the way she watched out for hers. 'Do you live with your dad? You should count your blessings that your father has allowed you to get on with living your life. An overprotective dad can be more of a curse than a blessing sometimes.'

'He lives nearby,' Luca murmured.

'Close enough to be a problem?' She raised her eyebrows and grinned.

'Close enough for me to keep an eye on him.' Luca's mouth twitched and he smiled back at her. The sandwiches, he thought, were bloody good. Wholesome. 'The truth is life might have been better if he'd done what your father did, and retreated, at least for a decent amount of time. Instead, my father has entered into marriages with alarming regularity and none of the endings have been good ones.'

'I'm getting the picture.' No wonder he was jaded, she thought with a spurt of sympathy. She rested her hand on his wrist and gave it a little squeeze. The feel of that touch sent an electric charge racing straight from his wrist to what was visibly stirring underneath the swimming trunks. He shifted uncomfortably, adjusting himself in the process.

Whatever picture she was getting, it certainly wasn't a complete one.

'It must have been a lonely time for you.'

Luca shrugged. 'I've never been lonely in my life.' He thought back with some fondness to the English boarding school he had attended for so many years. No, there had been no shortage of people in his life. Had he been lonely? He frowned, unwilling to give house room to that notion, which smacked of the sort of weakness he despised.

'Were you close to any of your…er…stepmothers? How many were there?'

'A few and no.' He settled back on his elbows and stared up at a blue, blue sky. 'I don't believe there was a stepmother who didn't turn out to be a piece of work. It's a blessing my father's been on his own for a couple of years now, although it might be a bit premature to say that he's seen the light.'

'You really love him, don't you? For all his failings. Just something else we have in common!'

Luca looked at her thoughtfully. 'Amazing,' he murmured, 'given the circumstances, that you are as upbeat and romantic as you are.'

'You think I should be cynical and jaded?'

'I've seen the trail of misery love has a habit of leaving in its wake. You call it cynical and jaded but I call it realistic. As far as I'm concerned, you look at life with your eyes wide open and you can escape most of its predictably unpleasant fallout.'

'Which is why you like the thought of an arranged marriage…'

'A suitable union between two people whose outlook on life is similar. Remind me why we're talking about all of this…?'

'Because it's nice getting to know someone else. I *know* you won't be around for much longer, but it's still nice getting to know you.'

When was he actually going to go? He'd extended this visit far longer than was technically acceptable. He was a workaholic and, of course, this unforeseen break in the normal course of events had been fun, but it couldn't continue.

And yet…he remembered the feel of her against him and his explosive reaction to her body, and the thought of jumping ship when he knew he should, which was just as soon as he could shove his clothes in a plastic bag and order a cab to the nearest airport, held little appeal.

'And believe me,' he murmured with heartfelt sincerity, 'I would certainly like to get to know you better as well.' It was a sign of creativity and a willingness to go with the flow that he was prepared to take a few more days out of his hectic schedule. In life, if something presented itself as a once-in-a-lifetime opportunity, you grabbed it with both hands. This was a once-in-a-lifetime opportunity.

He smiled slowly.

'Another week here isn't going to hurt…is it?' He reached forward and she leaned into him. He kissed her long and slow and Cordelia melted.

'Another week,' she sighed breathlessly, 'would be great.'

'And then we'll bid our fond farewells. Deal?'

Something inside her stirred and she tore her eyes away from the puzzling void that opened up when she thought about him leaving.

She smiled. 'Deal.'

CHAPTER FOUR

'OF COURSE IF you want to go, if you feel you need to leave me when things are so busy here, then I can't stand in your way. You're a grown woman, Cordelia. You can do whatever you want to do and I understand that you need to get away for a while. Don't blame you. What young thing wants to be cooped up with her old fool of a father?'

Under normal circumstances, Cordelia would have wilted under this flagrant emotional blackmail. Sitting across from her father at the pine table where they had just finished sharing a fraught supper, she took a deep breath, the sort of deep breath typical of someone determined to power on whatever the obstacles.

These were not normal circumstances and she didn't have the luxury of succumbing to Clive Ramsey's mournful blue eyes.

'One week at the very most, Dad.'

She glanced down to the chips slowly going cold

on her plate. She'd barely eaten. She shoved the plate to one side and leaned forward, elbows planted on the table.

Once upon a time, her father had been gloriously good-looking. A strapping man with the same white-blond hair as hers and light blue eyes. Time, grief and disappointments had changed all that and now, at the age of sixty-two, he was still lean and strong, but his face was lined, his hands gnarled from all the manual work he did, and his once erect frame was stooped. A tall man hiding away from life and it showed in the way he carried himself.

'One week?' He sighed and attempted a smile, which tugged every heartstring she had.

'I know you think that once I'm gone, I'm never going to come back, but that won't be the case.' Cordella thought of the trip she was about to make. If she lasted five minutes there, then she would be amazed. Nausea swamped her again and she shoved the plate with the now cold chips further away from her because the sight of the slowly congealing food was doing nothing for the state of her stomach.

Pregnant. How could it have happened? Her period, as regular as clockwork, had been ten days overdue before it had even occurred to her to do a pregnancy test. She had been living on her nerves ever since.

Luca had stayed on for a further week and then he had gone. The impact of his departure on her had been something she hadn't foreseen. Yes, she had assumed that she would miss him because they had shared such a wonderful three weeks together. He had blown a hole in her orderly, predictable life and she'd known that it would take a while for normality to paper over his absence.

But she hadn't expected the depth of those feelings of loss and wanting. She physically *ached* for him. She saw him in every room in the house and on every corner of every street in the little village, where he had become such a familiar sight that people asked after him when he'd gone.

And when she closed her eyes, his image took shape in her head with such clarity that she felt that if she tried hard enough, she would open her eyes and he would be there. Standing in front of her, so tall and so bronzed and so sinfully sexy.

He'd gone, though, and he hadn't looked back. Not a text, not an email, not a phone call. Nothing. He'd warned her that he was just passing through and he'd cautioned her about getting emotionally involved with him and she'd nodded and agreed and said all the right things and had promptly done just the opposite of what he'd asked.

She'd laughed in the face of common sense and flung herself into a one-sided relationship with a guy who didn't believe in love.

And now she was pregnant and it was like walking in a dense fog with her feet in treacle. Every thought about *what happened next* required such effort that she had spent the past few days just wanting to crawl into her bed and close her eyes and sleep for a hundred years.

As it had turned out, fate had had an excellent way of galvanising her into action. No taking time out to think things over! Or hiding under the duvet and pretending to be an ostrich!

'And I don't want you fretting that something's going to happen to me,' she said briskly, sweeping aside her fear of the big unknown and plastering a reassuring smile on her face.

Her father knew nothing about the pregnancy and that was something that she would broach in due course. When she reached the right levels of courage. That time was certainly not now.

'Things happen,' her father responded morosely. 'We both know that.'

'And we have to move on, Dad.' God, she missed having her mum. She adored her dad, with all his endearing, frustrating, lovable little ways, but, Lord, what she wouldn't have given for the emotional support of a mother, a hand to reach out and hold hers right now when she so desperately needed it.

'You're young. The wisdom of youth is fleeting. Take it from me. I'll say no more except that I'll miss you. Maybe you could leave a list of what needs to be done while you're away.'

'Ah.' She paused and waited until her father was

looking at her. 'There won't be any need for you to worry about anything while I'm away, Dad.'

'I'll be out fishing all day.' He frowned. 'The haul is good just at the moment. I won't have time to sort out that business with the rentals. And food. No, forget I said that. I can buy in some tins. Baked beans. Soup. You go and enjoy yourself, Cordy. You deserve it.'

Cordelia thought about the enjoyment lying in wait for her and shuddered. 'Dad—' she inhaled deeply '—you won't have to worry about food or the rental because Doris is going to take care of all of that for you.'

She waited for the explosion. She almost closed her eyes. Doris Jones was her father's arch enemy. Buxom, blonde and with a personality that could send strong men scurrying for cover, she had had her eye on Clive Ramsey's business for as long as Cordelia could remember.

'We could be a team,' she had ventured years ago. 'My three boats with yours. We could have ourselves a proper little business.'

Clive had been incandescent with rage at the barefaced cheek of the woman. There and then, she had become his nemesis. As fate would have it, nemesis was going to be taking charge while Cordelia was away, whether her dad liked it or not.

Of course, if he refused to oblige, she told him once he had finished ranting and raving, which made a change from his stoic, barely concealed gloom, she would ditch her plans and stay put…because he certainly wouldn't be able to cope on his own and she had no intention of spending her one week of the year when she should be relaxing worrying about him.

Cordelia knew that she was taking a gamble. If her father dug his heels in, then what was she going to do? Her ticket was all booked and even though this trip to Italy filled her with sickening apprehension, it was something that had to be done. For better or for worse, the guy who had vanished out of her life and hadn't looked back would have to be told about the baby he had never expected to father.

Her father caved in.

'It'll be fine.' She hugged him.

It'll be fine for at least one of us, at any rate.

'Don't think I haven't noticed you and Doris having a laugh now and again at the pub over a pint.'

Clive Ramsey flushed and he glared at his daughter. 'A man can't be rude all the time,' he countered defensively.

She'd won this round. There was no way she intended to let on to her father that she had found herself between a rock and a hard place when it came to Doris. If life were a fairy tale, she would laugh at the crazy coincidence of being caught red-handed emerging from a bathroom clutching a pregnancy-testing box by the one person who shouldn't have been anywhere near the area. But Doris had been there, larger than life and bursting with curiosity and she hadn't given up asking questions until she'd got the truth. Cordelia could only console herself with the thought that at least her father would be well fed, if nothing else. Doris was well known for her pies.

'So it's agreed, then…' She looked at him anxiously and she saw him visibly soften.

'I don't like it…'

'Those rentals need to be sorted. I know the timing's awful, but I had no idea…'

No idea that I was going to find myself carrying a child…that all that longing to see new places would end up as a nightmare journey to deliver a message that was definitely not going to brighten Luca Baresi's day…

'I had no idea that that problem would blow up like a squall, just after I'd booked to go away on the spur of the moment.'

'Well, Ireland isn't a million miles away, I suppose. And I know you've been wanting to do a little research into your mum's family tree.'

Cordelia didn't say anything but her fingers were tightly crossed behind her back.

She never ever lied and certainly would never have dreamt of lying to her dad, but the truth, laid bare, would have turned his already grey hair even greyer.

There was only so much she could deal with just at the moment and telling her father the whole truth and nothing but the truth, and then having to deal with the fallout, had felt like a step too far.

She smiled weakly. 'I promise it's going to be all right.' She was tempted to burst into manic laughter because from where she was sitting there was very little chance that anything was going to be all right in the foreseeable future. 'I'm going away and maybe we should both see that as the start of a changing future. For both of us. Maybe it'll do you good to not have me around. Now, I'm going to pack. I have a taxi booked to take me to the airport and it'll be coming very early, so I'll say goodbye now and poke my head in your bedroom in the morning if you're not already up.' She could see tears gathering in the corners of his eyes and her heart restricted.

She had to go. She'd meant what she'd said about changes. Everything was changing and for someone who had spent a lifetime harnessed to the yoke of duty and responsibility, the changes were terrifying.

The future was sprawled in front of her with a frightening lack of certainty. She'd spent her life yearning for what lay out there, beyond the small confines of the village where she lived, and now a door had been opened but for all the wrong reasons and what lay behind that door was not, she felt, going to be the wonderful adventure she had always hoped for.

One week, though, and she would have had the conversation she had to have, then she would be back, and at least she would have seen somewhere different, breathed in different air, looked at a different landscape.

She would have to keep her fingers crossed that she could handle everything that came in between.

'There's someone here asking for you.'

Luca looked up from where he had been scrolling through his emails on his computer to the elderly man who had ambled into his office without knocking and was now in the process of straightening everything on his desk, clucking disapprovingly under his breath.

'Roberto…' Luca controlled a sigh because the man had been a loyal retainer since the dawn of time and if he was now in his early eighties, with a meandering mind and prone to forgetting that there was an army of stalwart help paid to do what might once have been part of his job, then so be it. 'There's no need to tidy the desk. I know where everything is. At any rate, I'm busy so anyone wanting to see me will have to make an appointment through the usual channels.' He had two PAs. One handled matters of a more confidential nature, the other handled anything that required interfacing with non-Italian clients, of which there were very many.

PAs…hired help…three-course meals that appeared as if by magic…a social life that left very little free time, especially now that the presumption of nuptials with Isabella lay thick in the air, even though nothing had been formally announced. Recently he'd felt as though he had to make time in his packed diary to breathe.

He frowned and restlessly pushed himself away from his desk and waited until Roberto had straightened everything to his satisfaction.

'Never used to be that way,' Roberto responded, shaking his head sadly. 'There was always time for a face-to-face meeting. A chat. Everybody knew everybody. It was a family.'

'Times change.' Luca had heard all this before. Naturally, he couldn't interface with everyone who worked for him! His winery employed very many people, kept two villages in employment, practically! There wasn't a human being who could keep track of every single person who might show up unannounced on the doorstep. 'I haven't got time to see anyone at the moment. Now, is that all?'

'So I'll show her in, shall I?'

Luca flung both hands in the air and gave up. He had zero curiosity as to the identity of his visitor. Theoretically his door was always open to any of his employees. In practice, the door was largely shut and, when ajar, was ferociously guarded by PA number one, who made sure that his time was uninterrupted by anything of a remotely trivial nature. If it could be sorted outside the hallowed walls of his office, which sprawled across one of the wings of his grand house, then it was. Rosa saw to that. Sadly, Rosa was on a one week vacation and, for some reason, Luca had not wanted the annoyance of a temp because there was no way Sonya, his tri-lingual PA, could be spared to waste time for a week doing bits of grunt work.

Unfortunately, without Rosa around, Luca could see that irritating interruptions were not going to be headed off at the pass. At least, not if Roberto happened to be unofficial gatekeeper.

'Five minutes,' he huffed, all but tapping his watch to make sure Roberto got the message loud and clear. 'And then you're to come and remove whoever I happen to be with.'

'Very rude, sir, when someone is kind enough to call by for a chat.'

'But essential. *Five minutes*, Roberto!'

Luca had doubts as to whether these instructions would be obeyed. He would have to control the urge to snap were they to be ignored. His temper, always ruthlessly controlled, had been far too much in evidence ever since he had returned from that brief sojourn on the Cornish coast and he had no idea why.

What he *did* know was that the lack of control infuriated him.

He waited until Roberto had shuffled off and then he swivelled his chair to face the massive bay window, frowning and staring out towards a vista that was impressive by anyone's standards.

He barely noticed the mansion in which he lived. It was there. Ancient, beautiful, vast, handed down through the generations. Huge tracts of it were unused simply because there were so many rooms. Walls were adorned with exquisite paintings that were seldom seen. There were priceless rugs upon which no feet ever trod and windows were flung open in rooms simply to let in a bit of fresh air before they were shut again and those very rooms remained silent and empty until they were aired again.

His own quarters, done to the highest of standards, were far more modern, as was the four-bedroomed annexe in which his father lived when he wasn't travelling, as he was now, hopefully not on the lookout for another unsuitable wife. Personally, Luca couldn't abide the heaviness of all that traditional décor that characterised most of his estate but he didn't care enough to do anything about it.

It was his ancestry and that was the end of it.

He barely noticed any of it, but through this window...*that* was what he noticed.

The rolling acres of carefully cultivated grapevines, marching in lines towards a distant horizon, punctuated by tall, elegant cypress trees...the backdrop of hazy purple mountains rising so high in the distance that the peaks were blurred by cloud... the villages clinging to the sides of the hills, white squares against lush green.

He was staring out at the scenery when the door

was pushed open and, with a sigh of resignation, he slowly spun round to address whatever needed addressing.

For a few seconds, Luca only registered Roberto, who was hovering, eyeing up the desk with intent, resisting the urge to do a bit more tidying, then he stepped aside and...

He'd been relaxed back in the deep leather chair. Now Luca leant forward and every nerve and muscle in his body slowly stretched to breaking point. The woman was, naturally, registering in some part of his brain but even so his eyes were telling him that he couldn't possibly be seeing the leggy blonde with whom he had spent three weeks of unadulterated carefree pleasure.

It wasn't possible. For once in his life, Luca was rendered speechless and, in that brief period, Roberto pushed an obviously reluctant Cordelia into the room.

'Will tea or coffee be taken, sir?' he queried without a hint of irony, even though he had been banned from fetching and carrying three years previously after he had managed to drop an eye-wateringly expensive vase, which he had been lifting from its podium to dust. 'Some wine, perhaps?' His watery eyes glinted.

'Just close the door behind you, Roberto,' Luca managed to say. 'And no tea or coffee and certainly no wine at four in the afternoon. Thank you.'

He couldn't tear his eyes off the woman who was now pressed against the closed door. He was barely aware of drawing breath. His thought processes had been temporarily suspended and the most he could do was take in the rangy body that had been his undoing for three sensational weeks.

She was dressed in a pair of faded jeans and a loose red and white checked shirt. Her long hair was pulled back into a plait.

Luca's nostrils flared at the memory of that vibrant hair spilling over her shoulders, a tumble of gold and vanilla and every other shade of blonde imaginable. He recalled the electric charge that had raced through his body every time he had curled his fingers in its length, held her heavy breasts in his hands, nuzzled the soft down between her thighs and felt her writhe with passion under his touch.

'Well,' he drawled, lazing back in the chair, 'this is certainly a surprise.' And, he thought, an unwelcome one, never mind the trip down memory lane, which had the annoying effect of reminding him that he had a libido.

Luca was a pragmatist. He had known from the very first time he had touched her that what they had was not destined to go anywhere. Those three weeks had been enjoyable—no, that didn't come close to describing it, but it had been life lived in a bubble. He'd been completely free for the first time in his life and freedom had tasted sweet.

But this was his real life and never the twain should have met.

Displeasure flared inside him, partly because she had shown up here unannounced and now he would have to firmly but politely turn her away, and partly because there was a treacherous side of him that was *pleased* at her unexpected appearance. He realised that he'd been thinking about her, in a dark, subconscious sort of way, his thoughts titillating and illicit.

'How can I help you?' he pursued into the lengthening silence as she continued to hover.

Of course he knew why she was here and he wondered how she would broach the inevitable conversation. It was disappointing that it had come to this but not really that surprising. People were lamentably predictable in the ways they reacted to money.

Even her, and if it made his gut twist to wise up to the fact that she was no different from the next person, then that was his deal.

'Is it all right if I sit?' There was an empty chair in front of the desk and her legs were like jelly. If she didn't sit soon, she would end up crumpled in an undignified heap on the floor and she could tell from the lack of warmth on his face that he wouldn't be offering her tea and sympathy should that be the case.

Indeed, from the expression on his face, the last person he wanted to see at all was her.

The man staring at her with cool, assessing eyes

was a stranger. He bore no resemblance to the guy who had swept her off her feet and taken her to places she had never dreamed possible with his fingers, his hands, *his mouth*.

But then this guy bore no resemblance to the man she'd thought she'd find when she'd set off. He worked in a vineyard. He picked grapes. Then when the season was over, he travelled. He wasn't an itinerant, but neither was he...*this*.

She'd known where he worked and lived because he'd told her. She'd expected a modest dwelling, maybe shared with his father. Something modest but pretty. One of those whitewashed Mediterranean houses she'd seen in pictures over the years.

But when she'd asked after him, she'd been directed to this mansion. A lovely old woman with a crinkled face and black eyes as lively as a sparrow's had walked with her up the hill, with carefully tended vines falling away from them in rows down towards fields and trees. There had been no conversation. Cordelia didn't speak a word of Italian and the old lady, smiling and friendly as she was, spoke no English, so there had been no opportunity to ask what the heck was going on and why was she being taken to a vast stone fortress complete with turrets and surrounded by cypress trees.

The heat had been sapping and the pull-along had felt as heavy as lead by the time they had trudged in silence up the hill to stand in front of the fortress, which, on closer inspection, wasn't quite as coldly unwelcoming as she'd first thought.

There were shutters in the windows and colourful flowers spilling out in borders at the front.

And now here she was and if she didn't sit soon…

She didn't wait for him to signal the seat in front of him. She walked towards it, her troubled blue eyes skittering away from his closed, unwelcoming face.

He didn't want her here and it was beginning to dawn on her why that was the case.

Luca Baresi wasn't an ordinary guy. This wasn't the house of an ordinary man. Luca Baresi was a multimillionaire, and she wished that she'd had the common sense to look him up on the Internet before she'd packed her bag and made the trip to Italy.

But why, she asked herself feverishly, would she have done that?

She'd thought that he was a simple guy who worked in a vineyard in Italy. Simple guys didn't have profiles on the Internet.

'I guess you're surprised to see me,' she opened, clearing her throat.

'Less surprised than you might think.' Luca's voice was cool.

'I would have contacted you…phoned…but…' Her voice trailed off. She noticed that she was plucking compulsively at the checked shirt and she sat on her hands to stop.

'No phone number. I know. I didn't leave you with one.'

Cordelia flushed. He couldn't have made it any clearer that she was not welcome. She tilted her head at a combative angle and reminded herself that this trip had been voluntary. She was pregnant and she could very easily have not bothered to tell him. She was here for a reason and she'd be gone within the hour. Lord knew, a week seemed like a long time but maybe she would see a bit of Tuscany before she headed back home.

'No,' she said with equal cool. 'You didn't. Why would you when you spent three weeks lying to me? Of course, the last thing you would have encouraged would be any further contact from the country bumpkin you used for your own amusement and dumped. Heaven knows, my showing up here on your doorstep must seem like the worst of your nightmares.'

Luca had the grace to flush but he didn't say anything because there was no point launching into self defence.

'You said you weren't surprised to see me here,' Cordelia prompted icily. 'What did you mean?'

He shrugged eloquently and sat back, steepling his fingers under his chin, then clasping his hands behind his head to look at her from under thick dark lashes.

'You looked me up on the Internet,' he said flatly.

'Curiosity, no doubt. You discovered that I was not quite the person you thought I was.'

Cordelia could barely conceal her snort of disgust. She thought back to just how elegant, arrogant and self-confident he'd been. She'd naively put it down to his *foreignness*. Instead, those had just been the telltale traits of a man who lived in a castle and owned a million acres of vineyards. Lack of experience had not been her friend when it had come to making sense of his personality.

'Really?' she said, tight-lipped.

'Really. You would have struck jackpot on the first hit and I guess that got you thinking that what we'd enjoyed might have come to something of a premature end. Were you dazzled at the thought of continuing a relationship but this time with a man worth billions instead of a guy with only the clothes on his back and a seasonal job?' He paused, watched carefully for signs of guilt and embarrassment, and saw neither.

Luca raked his fingers through his hair and vaulted upright. The chair suddenly felt confining, the room too small.

'I'm a rich man,' he said, striding towards the window and looking out to everything he owned for a few seconds, before turning to face her. 'I know how the game is played.'

The sun was no longer high in the sky and its rays through the window emphasised the pale hue of her skin and the sprinkling of freckles across her short, straight nose. His lips thinned as he felt a familiar ache in his groin.

'So you think I've come here to offer myself to you because you have all *this*...'

'Of course you have!' He heard the softness of her laughter in his head, the lilt of her voice when they were in bed, talking quietly while he stroked her face. He clenched his fists because he didn't welcome those memories. They didn't belong here. 'But you've made your trip in vain, Cordelia. Naturally, I will compensate you for your travel. But return to Cornwall you must, because you don't, for a thousand reasons, belong here...'

CHAPTER FIVE

'A THOUSAND REASONS?' Cordelia enquired icily. She didn't think so. One reason and he had just said it in four simple words. *You don't belong here.*

Was this the opening she needed to take? Should she nod mutely and leave? Let him think that he had struck jackpot with his insulting, offensive and sweeping assumption?

She thought of her father. An honourable man. She'd inherited his sense of right and wrong. To walk away now without explaining why she had come in the first place…

What would that make her? In his eyes and in her own? She would know the truth and, of course, that should be all that mattered, but the very idea of leaving him with the mistaken impression that she was a seedy gold-digger willing to sacrifice herself for cash was too much to take in.

'Cordelia.' Luca's voice softened. 'You really don't understand…'

'I really think I do,' she returned, without skipping a beat. 'You think I've come here with a begging bowl. You think that the only reason I might have wanted to get in touch with you would be because I've found out how rich you are and what a catch you would be for a poor fisherman's daughter like myself.'

'Maybe that's just a part of the equation,' Luca murmured, simultaneously knowing that he should gently but firmly usher her to the door, see her on her way, yet, stupidly, finding that he couldn't quite bring himself to do it. Not just yet. 'And I mean no insult.'

'That's wonderful of you,' she said tightly. 'You mean no insult and yet you just happen to have insulted me in the worst possible way.'

'Of course I don't consider you a poor fisherman's daughter. As a matter of fact, I have a great deal of respect for your father. He is an honest man making an honest living. Believe me, I have spent my adult life seeing the corruption that all this can buy.' He gestured to encompass the vastness of his house and the enormous wealth it represented. 'Your father… I respect him…'

'Thank you,' Cordelia said politely, while, inside, she raged with the force of an erupting volcano at what she could only interpret as his smug contempt for everything she stood for. How on earth could she not have seen through him? 'I'll make sure I tell him.'

'Perhaps,' Luca murmured, watching the satiny softness of her skin, the tinge of colour spreading across her high cheekbones. He had to stop himself from staring. Worse, from closing his eyes and remembering the supple strength of her beautiful body, the fullness of her breasts, the smoothness of her inner thighs. 'Perhaps…' he dragged his thoughts away from those dangerous zones and back to the matter at hand, which was the necessity to show her to the door '…you really haven't come here because you'd sussed who I was and what I'm worth. It beggars belief that you would have taken this length of time to make your move, but were I to give you the benefit of the doubt…' he sighed and raked his fingers through his hair, annoyed because for once in his life the logical way forward with the conversation was not one he felt comfortable taking '…then the outcome would be the same. *Cara*, we had our moment in time, and believe me when I tell you that I will cherish it for ever, but it was no more than a moment in time.'

His words slithered through her like shards of glass, destroying every rose-hued memory. She felt sick. The ground seemed to be spinning under her feet and she took a few deep breaths and balled her hands into fists.

'My life here is prescribed,' he said softly. 'More

than I can begin to explain. These vineyards…' he signalled to the window, beyond which lay all those rows of carefully tended vines, heavy with grapes '…they are my legacy and I can no more escape my destiny than you can escape yours.'

'My destiny to remain where I was born? You mean *that* destiny?' Of course, that was what he meant. She'd told him all the ins and outs of her life, had lain in his arms and mused on all those doors that had been solidly closed for her. She'd laid bare her heartfelt wish that she could see the world, see what was out there. God, was it any wonder that, with her having shown up on his doorstep, he'd instantly jumped to all sorts of conclusions?

'You have always wanted to see the world. If you have not researched me, if you truly arrived here thinking that you would find the impoverished manual worker you imagined me to be, then you have my most sincere apologies. It would make sense that you might find yourself tempted to cross the ocean to make contact with someone who might represent an escape from your life, which is as prescribed as my own…'

Cordelia tilted her head to one side. She was curious to see how far he would run with this particular theory. It wasn't quite as offensive as theory number one, but nevertheless it still felt like a kick in the teeth after all the things they had shared.

After all the things, she mentally amended, *she*

had shared. He'd just sat back and done the taking. And, of course, *the lying*.

'But, as I said, for very many reasons, what we have is no more and cannot be resurrected.' He looked down, lush dark lashes concealing his expression.

'Of course,' Cordelia expanded coolly, 'as you mentioned, I don't belong here.'

'Cordelia, it's slightly more than that.'

'What more could there be, Luca?' She paused and looked at him in stony silence. 'If I'm not a gold-digger, then I'm a sad, love-struck ex who was so desperate to live a little that she decided to show up, unannounced, on the doorstep of a guy who walked away from her without a backward glance. I don't know which is worse. Oh, no. I *do* know. They're both bad.'

'I am destined to marry a woman I have known from my childhood.' Why bother going round the houses? He watched as the colour drained away from her face.

'You're *engaged*?'

'Not as such.' Luca flushed darkly and looked away from her accusing gaze.

'What does that mean?'

'It is an understanding.'

'I see.' It was a mistake coming after all. He was engaged to be married. The outcome couldn't have been worse for her. To be faced with a baby bombshell would be his ugliest nightmare and she couldn't do that to him. The giddiness was growing and the spinning in her head made her want to close her eyes but she gritted her teeth together and remained present.

'I don't think you do.'

'You're going to be married and yet you led me to believe…you let me think…'

'No rings were exchanged. You misunderstand.'

'I don't believe I do.'

'It was always an understanding between families. A marriage of convenience. Isabella belongs to a dynasty like mine and the union would secure an estate of unimaginable wealth.'

'Right. What could be better than that? Who, in their right mind, would refuse unimaginable wealth?'

Luca shook his head in frustration. 'You're not getting it. I…when you met me, I was in a weird place. I knew that the time for this marriage was fast approaching but I was reluctant to commit to that final step. I needed to think.' He pressed the pads of his thumbs against his eyes and then looked at her wearily.

For a second, just a second, Cordelia could sense his confusion and she felt a tug of sympathy for a man trapped by his elevated birth, more trapped than she had ever been, then her sympathy vanished and she hardened her jaw because she was in an impossible situation and he had lied to her.

'And do you…love her?'

'Love? What are you talking about?'

'I'm just asking a question.'

'Love has nothing to do with this arrangement,' Luca said matter-of-factly.

'Poor woman.'

'Isabella?' His voice held surprise.

'Does she know what she's letting herself in for?'

'We are tremendously well suited.' They were. They looked the part and they certainly belonged together. That was a given.

Yet his thoughts sped back to those heady three weeks when he had been just an ordinary person with no expectations weighing on his shoulders, free to enjoy life in all its wonderful simplicity. Free to enjoy the woman staring at him as though she didn't quite recognise the man sitting in front of her.

Cordelia was hearing him but she had stopped taking in precisely what he was saying.

He was getting married. There were no rings on fingers yet, but he was getting married and he'd known that when they had slept together. He had truly only seen what they'd enjoyed as something passing and she knew that, while she had said all the right things, while she had assured him that she, likewise, knew the rules of the game, in her heart she had started hoping for more.

Maybe he didn't love the woman whose finger was destined to wear his ring, but they were tremendously well suited. Cordelia wasn't sure quite what that meant, but there had been affection in the tenor of his voice and affection was only a heartbeat away from love.

At any rate, it was a heck of a lot more than he felt *for her*. She thought of the baby she was carrying.

In her enthusiasm to get to Italy and tell Luca about the pregnancy, Cordelia had not been thinking straight and she could see that now. She'd never, of course, thought that Luca might have been lying to her. She'd also, she now realised with dismay, nurtured a certain excitement about seeing him again, even though he hadn't glanced back in her direction. She'd cherished the wild hope that they might recapture what they'd had, that he might actually *want* the baby she was carrying. She'd been swept away by happy-ever-after fantasies and now that all those fantasies had been exposed for what they were, she was desperate to leave.

She was going to keep this secret to herself. She would never hide his identity from the child they shared and in due course, if he or she wanted to meet him, then she wouldn't prevent it. By that time Luca would be happily married and a child he had sired as a youthful mistake before getting married would not be the catastrophe it would be now.

She stood up, keen to leave, thoughts in a confusing, sickening muddle, and felt the ground sway gently under her.

She held the back of the chair to steady herself and was vaguely aware of him shooting to his feet as she turned away, eyes fixed on the door.

'Cordelia…!'

When she looked up it was to find him standing right in front of her, his eyes filled with concern.

'You're as white as a sheet.' He placed his hands on her arms and she shrugged them off but she didn't say anything because her mouth was refusing to co-operate. 'Look at me,' he commanded, tilting her head so that she had no option but to do as he'd asked although her eyes, when they met his, were muti-nous. 'I want you to sit back down. Have you eaten anything in the last few hours? I get that all this will be a shock to you but there was no point in keeping anything back, in giving you false hope.'

'Leave me alone, Luca. I just want to go. I should never have come here in the first place.'

'If things had been different…' he said roughly.

'If things had been different…*what*, Luca?'

'The time we spent together was special to me.'

'I'm thrilled to hear that,' Cordelia told him acidly. The swaying had stopped but she still felt giddy, as though she'd been flying on a roller coaster and now the ride had stopped but her head was still spinning.

He had softened his hold on her and as their eyes tangled he gently and absently began to massage her shoulder with his hand, slow rhythmic motions that shot straight to every nerve ending in her body with devastating effect. Her eyes widened in horror at her treacherous body and she began to take a step back to break the connection that had sprung up between them, but she just couldn't seem to do it. Her feet were nailed to the ground. It was a struggle to do anything. Breathing was proving a problem, never mind anything else.

'I have never been the man I was with you, with any other woman,' he said in a roughened undertone. 'I have never *wanted* any other woman the way I wanted you.' His eyes dropped to her full mouth and the connection she was desperately trying to sever took on a life force of its own.

He traced the outline of her mouth with the tip of his finger and she breathed in sharply

He was going to kiss her. She could feel it in the simmering intensity of his gaze. It was the last thing she wanted! She opened her mouth to protest and her whole body shuddered as his lips touched hers, gently at first but then with increasing hunger.

Cordelia curved against him. His lean, hard muscularity felt so wonderfully familiar. He'd been her first and only lover and she had traced the contours of his perfect body with such awe that he used to laugh at her enthusiasm.

It took more willpower than she knew she even possessed to flatten her palms against his chest and detach herself from his devouring caress.

She was shaking when she stepped back. She

could barely look him in the eye and he seemed to have as much of a problem holding her gaze. As he should, she thought bitterly. She'd succumbed to a moment of uncontrollable desire but she was free, single and unattached. It went utterly against the grain but she wasn't the one about to go shopping for engagement rings!

'I have to go,' she half muttered.

'I still want you.'

'You're practically married!' She flung him a look filled with accusation.

What did his fiancée-to-be look like? she wondered. It was an arranged marriage, if he was to be believed, and who could believe a guy who'd lied once? She drew some comfort from the thought that the woman in question might just be nothing much to look at and then hated herself for allowing her thoughts to travel down that uncharitable route.

Since Luca could hardly deny that reality, he maintained a tactful silence. The taste of her mouth was still on his, though, sending his thoughts into wild disarray. He didn't want to notice anything about her but he was noticing everything, from the slight tremor rippling through her long body to the strands of white-blonde hair escaping to brush against her cheek. He wanted to touch so badly that he had to bunch his hands into fists to stop himself from reaching forward.

'Are you in love with her?' Cordelia whispered,

hating the way she wanted an answer to that question, even if the answer might be as painful as having a knife twisted in her gut.

Luca remained silent. Where was the point in going down this road? It was as it was.

'That question is inappropriate,' he finally said, when she continued to look at him with huge, accusing, wounded eyes.

Cordelia shrugged. The giddy feeling was sweeping over her again. Of course he loved the woman. He just didn't want to come right out and admit it because to do so would have been conclusive proof of the cad he really was and there wasn't a man in the world who would voluntarily have chosen to hang that description round his neck if he could avoid doing so.

The picture building in her head was not an attractive one.

He'd gone sailing in his expensive toy on one last adventure as a free man before he tied the knot. She'd happened to walk slap bang into his path and he'd thought... *Why not?*

She'd utterly and completely misread him. She knew that she could no longer weakly try and give him the benefit of the doubt. The fact that he refused to deny that the woman he was betrothed to marry was more than just a convenient wife said it all.

She had to get out of his great big palace of a

house because it was pressing down on her, making her feel nauseous.

She thought of the baby inside her and the utter mess she had walked into and suddenly, without warning, she could feel herself falling and it was the most peculiar sensation.

It was as though she had left her body and was looking down at herself. Looking at the way her legs began to weaken and her eyes began to droop and her shoulders slumped and then her whole body went limp and slowly, oh, so slowly, she crumpled to the ground like a marionette whose strings had been cut.

He caught her before she hit the ground. Even as she briefly lost consciousness, she was aware of his arms around her waist and of him carrying her urgently over to a sofa.

Her eyes fluttered open and she shrank back because he was so close to her that the smell of him filled her nostrils and made her feel faint all over again.

'You're in shock,' he said. She began sitting up and he gently kept her still, his eyes anxiously scanning her face. 'You're not going to be getting up just yet. I don't want you fainting again.'

'I never faint.'

'I'm going to argue with that statement, considering I've just caught you before you hit the ground. Wait here. I'll be back in five.' He vaulted to his feet but stayed where he was for a few seconds, as though making sure she obeyed him.

Much as Cordelia wanted to run as fast as she could to the door and then make a bolt for it, she felt as weak as a kitten.

She was in shock. He was right. She sighed and lay back, closing her eyes and blocking out the sight of his tall, commanding figure.

She only opened her eyes when she heard the soft pad of his returning footsteps. In his hand he carried a glass of amber liquid and he positioned himself on the very edge of the sofa and gently placed his hand under the nape of her neck.

'You need to drink this.'

'What is it?' she whispered.

'Brandy. It'll do the trick.'

Cordelia whipped her head to one side.

'Drink it, *cara*. It'll make you feel better and then I'll make sure you have a bed here for the night. I know this is probably not the outcome you envisaged when you began your trip over here, but…like I said…'

'I'm not drinking any of that stuff.'

'For God's sake. I'm trying to *help* you. You're deathly white!'

'I can't drink it!' The words were out before she could claw them back and he stared at her, puzzled.

'Why not?'

'Because…it wouldn't be a good idea…'

'Why not?'

'Because I'm pregnant.'

She hadn't meant to say that. She'd decided, just as soon as she'd heard about his soon-to-be engagement to the woman who came from the same background as him and was his perfect match, that silence was the only option, but here, on his sofa, with legs like jelly, staring at a glass of brandy, the admission could not be stopped.

Maybe in her heart, she thought, she'd come to tell him about the pregnancy and she would have ended up doing so, whatever the circumstances.

A silence, thick with unspoken questions, settled between them as he stared at her with narrowed, incredulous eyes.

He wasn't taking any of it in and she could hardly blame him. In all those scenarios he had concocted explaining why she had travelled to Italy, none of them had touched on what should have been a likely contender.

'I'm sorry. I don't think I heard what you just said.'

'I'm sorry, Luca. I didn't come over here to try and resurrect a relationship with you because I discovered you had money and I didn't come to resurrect it because I stupidly decided that I just couldn't live another minute without you. I apologise if I've dented your ego. I came because I found out that I was pregnant a few days ago and I thought I owed it to you to tell you that you were going to be a father.'

The silence continued to coalesce. She couldn't look at him. She didn't want to see the horror there.

'You're lying,' Luca said hoarsely. 'That can't be…true.'

Cordelia sneaked a glance. He was ashen. He was also staring at her but she could tell that he wasn't really seeing her. He was seeing the nightmare scenario in his head. She watched as he sprang back to begin pacing the room, his movements, for once, lacking their usual grace.

Still muggy, she heaved herself into a sitting position and took a few deep breaths to steady herself.

His restless pacing was making her dizzy and yet, while he was walking, he wasn't talking and she dreaded hearing the dark, disbelieving and horrified timbre of his voice.

'I don't believe you,' he finally said, pausing to stand in front of her, then dragging a chair towards the sofa so that he could sit, interrogation style, directly in her line of vision. 'You can't be. We…were careful. We took all the necessary precautions. This can't be true.' He narrowed his eyes and stared at her and she could almost see the way his mind was working, shying away from the truth, finding other paths to follow.

She wasn't entirely surprised when he said,

bluntly, 'Is this some kind of ploy to get money out of me? Because if it is, then it's not going to work.'

'We're back to that, are we?'

'A fake pregnancy is the oldest trick in the book.' But she wasn't lying. Luca knew that in the very depth of his being. She wasn't like that. She was achingly honest and if she had travelled all this way to tell him that she was carrying his baby, then carrying his baby she was.

Right in front of him, the world was falling apart at the seams.

'Remember that first time?' Cordelia asked. She felt too tired to argue with him about whether she was pretending to be pregnant or not. It was ridiculous that he would even allow his thoughts to travel along those lines but, then again, who was to say how he really thought? Who he really was?

'I remember.'

'We were on the beach. Well, we weren't exactly careful then, were we?'

'I… Jesus… I… We… No, *I* took chances. I took a chance.' He flushed darkly as he relived every second of that mind-blowing experience. He'd been so turned on—and she'd been lying there, as tempting as a siren and he'd thought…that he would get away with it. No, that was a lie. The truth was that he hadn't thought at all. Her tightness had wrapped around his erection, rubbing it into a frenzied state of arousal, and he had exploded inside her.

His groin ached as he thought about it and he could feel his libido shoot into the stratosphere without warning.

Utterly inappropriate.

'You show up here, out of the blue…naturally, I would want confirmation…'

Cordelia shrugged. 'Why would I come all the way over here to lie to you about something like that? Don't you think that it's something that could be easily disproved if I were making it all up? One trip down to the local chemists would be all it would take.' She sighed and cast her eyes around the lavish room, so in keeping with the lavishness of the house and the stunning splendour of the limitless vineyards stretching into the blue horizon.

The giddiness had eased and her mind felt clear for the first time since she had found out that she was pregnant.

'What happened between us was a mistake,' she told him quietly. He was so ridiculously good-looking that she could barely allow her gaze to settle on him for too long. Look for too long and her mind started playing cruel tricks on her, started travelling down memory lane, and that was never going to do. 'You swept into my life and I guess it was just the extraordinary nature of the circumstances that brought you there, and the fact that you were so…so different from everyone and everything I'd ever known, that combined to undermine all the principles I'd lived by. I'd longed for adventure and, suddenly, there you were, just about as adventurous as they came. I admit that I was a little sad when you left, Luca...' she paused and took a deep breath, making sure that, whatever happened, she left with her dignity intact '...but not sad enough to come all the way over here in an attempt to seduce you back into a relationship.'

Luca scowled. Contained in that explanation was an insult although he couldn't quite put his finger on it, or on why he should feel so piqued.

'So you said.'

'It's understandable,' she mused softly. 'You were my first lover.'

'Your *first lover*?' Luca wanted to scoff, because, in his world, virgins were as rare as hen's teeth, but then he remembered the feel of her, that tightness. And more than that, he remembered what she had been like, skittish and shy, giving and then retreating, at once eager and timid. 'I would have known.'

'There's no point talking about that.' She waved aside his interruption. 'I came here because I thought you ought to know. I never expected to find what I did and I certainly never thought that I would be sitting here, explaining this situation to a guy about to tie the knot.'

Luca shifted uncomfortably. He thought of Isabella and the neatly parcelled future that had been lying in store for him.

'This is a mess,' he muttered.

Cordelia reddened. 'Not for you,' she said coolly. 'How so?'

'I'm not asking anything of you. I plan on going back to Cornwall and, of course, if you ever want to come and see your child, then you would be welcome, but that's as far as it goes when it comes to my expectations of you.'

'You're kidding, right?' he said incredulously.

'No, Luca, I'm not. In fact, the minute I heard that you were about to get married...'

'No one's bought a hat yet! Isabella has always been destined to be my wife. I am now thirty-four years old and the time has come. At this point it is an understanding rather than an arrangement with a fixed date.'

'Whatever. The fact remains that the minute you told me about...about... Isabella...' she could barely get the name out '... I made up my mind to leave without saying anything at all, but then I fainted and when you offered me that brandy, I thought of the baby and out it all came.' She shifted. 'But I don't intend to stick around here, *messing up* your life. I'm going to head back home and, like I said, you can do whatever you want to do.' She began getting to her feet.

'You're not going anywhere,' Luca gritted.

'I'm fine. I won't be fainting again, trust me. I'm as strong as an ox.'

'Repeat, you're not going anywhere. You don't

get to drop a bombshell in my life and then tell me that you're going to walk away as though nothing's happened.'

'I don't like the word *bombshell*.'

'And I'm not particularly in love with the notion of being a daddy in nine months' time, but there we have it. You're going to sit back down and we're going to discuss what happens next in this scenario.' His eyes involuntarily flickered to her stomach.

Fatherhood had always been something vague on the horizon. Naturally, he would have a child, preferably a son. It would all be part of the destiny lying in wait for him. Marriage to Isabella and the uniting of two great Italian families. Then a child, an heir to the throne, so to speak. Like him, Isabella would do what was expected and nothing beyond that. They were both very well aware of the circumstances of their individual situations and accepting of it. They were on the same page when it came to their future.

All pre-planned, laid out with precision. No room for emotion. It was the way he liked it anyway. He didn't believe in getting carried away. Love, and all the disorderly chaos it entailed, had never been for him. He'd seen too much and witnessed too much. Nothing good ever came from yielding to emotion and allowing it to carry you away until you became a helpless object, drifting wherever it decided to take you. His father had allowed emotion to dictate his life. His ex-wives…the constant upheavals…the shouting and crying and then the vindictiveness born from relationships gone sour. Too much.

And then his mother. He thought of his mother. He thought of the hole she had left in his father's life. And in his own. He would never revisit any situation that could put him in that distressing and vulnerable place again. If he could control his emotions, he could control his life. Control. That was what Isabella would bring to the table. He knew where he stood with her.

The woman looking at him in stubborn silence was the very opposite of Isabella. She'd brought out something in him that had been free and reckless and unchained and there was no place for that man here, in Italy. That man belonged back in Cornwall.

Did she think that she would find that man again? If so, she was very much mistaken. The Luca Baresi who lived here was not that man, which didn't mean that he could cheerfully send her on her way, not now that she had lit that fuse under him, a fuse that would spark a fire that would gobble up everything he knew and every plan he had ever made.

'I told you—' Cordelia began.

'I heard every word you said,' he murmured smoothly, 'and now you're going to hear every word I have to say.'

CHAPTER SIX

'First of all I will need to have the pregnancy confirmed. I have a trusted doctor.'

'I don't see the point. I'm not lying and I don't want anything from you. If you choose to disbelieve me, then that's okay. I will have done what I came to do and I'll leave here with a clear conscience.' She burned with curiosity about this woman he had chosen to be his future wife. Were they lovers? She didn't want to let her mind drift down those disturbing paths but she couldn't block out images of him with another woman. Her hormones were all over the place and just thinking those thoughts brought the sting of tears to her eyes.

'Provided there is a confirmed pregnancy, the announcement of our marriage will…not be a straightforward affair.'

Cordelia's mouth fell open and she stared at him in astonishment. He didn't notice. He was frowning, thinking, calculating. She realised that he was working out how to deal with the mess that had landed on his lap.

But *marriage*?

'I will have to convene a family meeting,' he continued, still seemingly oblivious to her gaping incredulity. He was thinking aloud and she could have been a potted plant in the corner of the room for all the attention he was paying to her. She was a problem that had to be addressed and he was in the process of addressing it.

'"Convene a family meeting"?' she asked, when in fact the question on the tip of her tongue was, *Marriage? Are you insane? What on earth are you talking about?*

'Firstly, I will, of course, have to break the news to my father.'

It struck Luca that his father was probably not going to hit the roof, contrary to what everyone else might expect. He knew his father. Giovanni Baresi, like the entire Russo clan, of whom Isabella was one of four daughters, expected him to marry into the other great Italian winery. Celebrations might not be afoot just yet but once the expected announcement was made, and everyone knew that that time was just round the corner because neither he nor Isabella were getting any younger, then preparations would move swiftly and smoothly. The wedding of the decade would be arranged with the exquisite perfection of a highly organised military campaign.

His father had talked about this arranged marriage recently, before departing on his extended holiday. There had been pressure but the pressure had been slight.

An arranged marriage. What suited him from an emotional point of view, not to mention financial point of view, was, deep down, anathema to a man like Giovanni Baresi, who had always enjoyed the highs and lows of an emotional-roller-coaster personal life. His great love had died too young but that had not stopped him from searching for its replacement in every unsuitable nook and cranny.

It had been enough to turn Luca off the whole messy business of falling in love for ever, which was something he suspected his father had never really understood.

So to have the news broken to him that his son had got a girl pregnant because he had been careless, had behaved out of character, would probably bring a sheen to the old man's eyes.

Luca would have to quench any romantic visions his father might have with brutal finality.

Then he would have to break the glad tidings to Isabella and finally to her parents.

Then the whole world would know and another, different life would begin for him.

He thought of Cornwall and the free, wild girl without make-up and he wondered how she would cope with life in Italy. He concluded, before that thought could go anywhere, that she would cope just fine because she would have limitless supplies of money and that always oiled the nuts and bolts of any discomfort.

He focused on her and narrowed his eyes because she was hardly looking as though she'd won the lottery.

'This won't be running along the normal lines,' he informed her with clipped gravity. 'There is a lot of unravelling that will have to take place. Unpicking expectations will always be a nightmare and expectations about my eventual nuptials with Isabella have long been embedded. Naturally, there will be disappointment all round. Tell me, how did your father take the news?'

Cordelia hadn't managed to squeeze a word out. Her head was buzzing. She felt as though she'd been whipped into some other parallel universe, the rules of which she didn't know and the scenery was not one with which she was familiar.

'My father?' she parroted weakly, clinging to the one thing he'd said that made any sense.

'Was he…surprised? I don't suppose…' Luca had the grace to flush '…it was what might have been expected of you.'

'He…he doesn't know.' She blushed and looked away.

'I'm sorry,' Luca said gruffly and her eyes shot towards him.

She heard the rough sincerity in his voice and for a

split second remembered the guy she had given herself to. He hadn't been this cold-eyed stranger. He'd been the guy who had just told her that he was sorry.

'Don't be. Things happen. You can't always predict the future.' She cleared her throat. His gaze on her was making her uncomfortable, reminding her of sensations that were no longer appropriate. She sternly told herself that it was precisely because of how he had made her feel that she had ended up here.

'Actually,' Luca confessed, 'I've always prided myself on being able to do just that.'

'In which case, I should be the one apologising.'

'For leading me astray?' His eyebrows shot up and the taut cast of his features relaxed into something approaching a smile. 'As they say, it takes two to tango and I was very much a willing dance partner.'

A sudden sense of danger rippled through her. The hairs on the back of her neck were standing on end and there was a tingle between her legs, a shameful feminine awareness that felt utterly inappropriate given the circumstances.

'I…' She cleared her throat to get a grip and directed her thoughts to her poor dad, who had been handed over to the safekeeping of his arch nemesis, Doris. 'I plan on telling him when I…get back…'

'This situation is pretty messy for both of us, isn't it?' Luca said quietly. 'How did you manage to get away? I was under the impression that he had quite a hold over you.'

Cordelia shot Luca a wry look from under her lashes. When they weren't talking about the pregnancy, she could feel herself noticeably relax even though asking about her father wasn't so much changing the subject as circling around it.

'I...it's a long story.'

'I'm all ears.'

'One of the women in the village happened to be in the very same chemist's a million miles away from home where I went to buy a...er...test. I didn't want to be spotted by anyone I knew and there was no way I could go to the local pharmacy, not unless I wanted the news to be shouted from the rooftops before I got to the end of the street.'

'And as luck would have it...?'

Cordelia nodded. Their eyes met and for a few seconds, neither looked away. Her heart was thumping like a sledgehammer and a fine perspiration had broken out all over her. She wanted to tear her eyes away but she couldn't and, in fact, he was the one to break eye contact, a dark flush spreading over his high cheekbones as he did so.

'As luck would have it,' she repeated breathlessly. She sucked in some air and steadied herself. 'The thing is, Doris isn't just any old nosey parker. She's had her eye on teaming up with Dad for ages, years, and she used the opportunity when she realised what was going on to nudge her way past the front door.'

'Surely you could have laughed and told her that it was for someone else.'

'I could have but I guess I just wasn't thinking straight at the time. I was so nervous. Petrified, as a matter of fact.'

Luca didn't say anything. He'd made a deal of his own life being irrevocably altered. He'd used expressions that she had found objectionable. Yet she, likewise, was facing the same life-changing event but had risen above the negativity to a place of acceptance.

Right now, he didn't feel great about himself but how was he to suspect, when she walked through that door, the reason for her sudden appearance? And it was perfectly understandable, surely, if he happened to be a bit tactless in his summary of the situation, given the fact that he had had zero time to digest what she had come to tell him.

And yet...

Something about the purity of her gaze and the wrenching honesty of her approach shamed him.

'There's no need to be petrified,' he murmured as he settled into the idea of a different life from the one to which he had resigned himself.

For one split second, he felt something that almost resembled elation, then it was gone, replaced by a far more prosaic take on what was unfolding in front of him. The horror, he had to admit, had subsided. He could only conclude that this was what was meant by thinking on your feet and adapting to a situation that had sprung from nowhere and wasn't going to go away. There would be consequences, not least the financial ones that would have benefited the union of two great wine-producing houses, but he would face those down and, more importantly, he would do so without grudging resentment. He would man up. He was good at that. He'd been doing it since he was a kid, when his mother had died and he'd been left in a wilderness.

'At least, not now.'

'You mean…' The weird marriage conversation began replaying in her head and she stared at him.

'Tomorrow, I will begin the process of breaking the news to all parties concerned.'

'Luca, no.' Cordelia felt that she had to interject before he got carried away. 'I didn't come here looking for…for that kind of solution.' She thought of the mysterious, wonderfully suited fiancée he had conveniently failed to tell her about and, just in case he started getting all the wrong ideas, added, 'We both agreed that what we had was just something that happened in the moment. We both agreed that we weren't, fundamentally, suited to one another. I know things have changed with this…situation…but it doesn't mean that we have to start thinking about getting hitched, because we don't. I am very happy for our child to have an ongoing relationship with you, which doesn't mean that *I* have to as well. And marrying you isn't going to do anything for my apprehension levels. You're not a knight in shining armour riding in on a white stallion to save me.'

'*Cara*, there is no option, I'm afraid.'

Cordelia stared at him and wondered how she'd managed to miss just how old-fashioned he must be, because no one in this day and age thought that a pregnancy had to be accompanied by a walk down the aisle.

Even in the village where she lived, Marsha Hall had had her baby out of wedlock and not too many eyebrows had been raised.

'What do you mean?'

'Maybe in your world,' he said gently, 'it is acceptable for a woman to have a baby while simultaneously relegating the father of the baby to the nearest wayside bin, but that's not how it works in my world.'

'Whoever said anything about wayside bins?' Cordelia questioned faintly.

'Provided, of course, that everything checks out, you will be having my baby and my baby will become the heir to...' he looked around him in the manner of a warrior casually surveying the fruit of his many conquests '...all of this. As an only child, it fell upon me to take up the mantle of responsibility, to do as duty dictated, and so it will be for my son. Or daughter, of course.'

'Sorry, but there are two of us involved in this equation, Luca. This child isn't exclusively *yours* and it's not a given that his or her future is to patiently do as told because that's what duty demands! Besides...' she narrowed shrewd eyes on his lean, handsome face '...weren't you trying to run away from all that wonderful duty of yours when you got caught out in that storm?'

Luca had the grace to flush. 'I don't like the term *run away*.'

'You know what I mean.' Cordelia clicked her tongue impatiently.

'I was having a bit of time out from my responsibilities. Everyone needs a holiday now and again.'

'It wasn't *a holiday*, Luca. Holidays are those things people take when they want to kick back and, most of the time, they don't involve doing a disappearing act from the rest of the world and then faking their identity so that they don't get caught out. Holidays are things that are booked in advance and everyone knows about them.'

'Since when did you get so argumentative?'

'Do you want to think about any child of yours being so harnessed to a yoke of responsibility that the only way to escape it is to disappear on a boat in the middle of the ocean where there are no prying eyes and no one telling them what needs to be done next?'

'There is a lot of exaggeration in that statement,' Luca said stiffly.

'I don't have the same aims as you, Luca, and I

don't like to think that any child of mine would have the same aims as you.'

'We're going to be married, Cordelia. My child… *our* child is going to be born into the Baresi family.'

'You're not being reasonable.' Cordelia could hear the slight tremor in her voice. She had come here to deliver a message. She hadn't dwelled on what the outcome of that message might be. Maybe, deep down, she had romantically dreamed of him telling her how much he'd missed her, welcoming the news about the baby, seeing it as an opportunity to resume what they had so prematurely brought to an end. She would, naturally, express misgivings. After all, he *had* walked away from her without looking back, but he would persist and she would succumb.

Admittedly, the daydreams had been unbelievably rosy hued, but even in those rosy-hued daydreams she had never thought that he would propose to her and certainly not a proposal as an arrangement, not unlike the nature of the one he had earmarked for his childhood sweetheart, if that was what she had been. He had been ready to marry for money, whichever way you looked at it, but then she had come along with news of a pregnancy and now he was ready to marry for the sake of the baby.

Luca Baresi did marriages of convenience but he didn't do marriages based on love and that was what her hungry, romantic heart craved. Since when had it ever been her dream to be someone's convenient bride?

'When I marry,' she murmured huskily, 'I want it to be for love.'

'Life is full of unfulfilled dreams.' Luca shrugged. 'I find it pays to adhere strictly to reality. You will have to break the news to your father and I will understand if you want to do so face to face, but can I trust you to return to Cornwall and not refuse to come back here? Probably not, which is why I will be more than happy to make arrangements for him to join us out here.' Luca paused. 'Rest assured he will travel in the very best possible style.'

'He can't leave his work!' Cordelia gasped. 'Nor would he want to!'

'Then you'll have to relay the news over the telephone.'

'You can't hold me prisoner here.'

'Is that what you think I would be doing?'

'What else, Luca?'

'Let's focus on one thing at a time, *cara*.' He flipped his mobile phone out and dialled, speaking in rapid Italian, not a word of which Cordelia understood. That, in itself, only served to make her feel even more disoriented. When the call was over, he sat back and looked at her with a shuttered expression.

'Tomorrow,' he announced, 'we will visit my consultant. Only then will any serious conversations begin...'

Within twenty-four hours, Cordelia realised that by *serious* Luca had actually meant *boardroom-formal*.

She had shown little resentment at having to prove to Luca what she knew to be the case. She was pregnant. She could have suggested taking a simple test—another one—but if he wanted to involve a consultant, then he would whether she did a thousand tests or not.

Along with the fact that he was not the man he'd said he was, she was discovering all kinds of sides to his personality that had not been at the forefront when they had had their brief, heady affair.

He was stubborn, proud, ridiculously traditional. He was also a man who expected to get exactly what he wanted and what he wanted was his child, with her as the price he would pay to achieve that.

The second the pregnancy had been confirmed, he had ushered her out into the fading sunshine, straight into the passenger seat of his low, sleek sports car and from there directly back to his mansion. Nothing had been said on the drive. He'd been thinking. She could sense that. As for the direction of his thoughts... Cordelia could only guess but, whatever she'd come up with, she had a suspicion that it would only cover part of the ground.

She'd reminded herself that it didn't matter what he was thinking because he couldn't force her to do anything she didn't want to do, and what she didn't want to do was marry a guy for all the wrong reasons.

Still, her stomach had been tightly clenched with nerves by the time they had arrived back at his house and he'd ushered her through the front door and into a kitchen that was as big as a ballroom and just as grand.

Had she decided about her father? he'd asked. Bring him over or deliver the news via phone? He would give her a night to mull it over and to digest the direction her life would now be taking. She was free as a bird to explore every nook and cranny of the house. It was, however, late. He would instruct the resident housekeeper to deliver her food to her bedroom. He, meanwhile, had phone calls to make but he would see her first thing in the morning for breakfast and they would begin their discussions about the future they would now be sharing.

If he had hoped to soothe her frayed nerves, he'd definitely gone about it the wrong way. She had barely been able to enjoy the lavish pasta meal that had been delivered to her door at a little after eight by a shy young girl who had practically genuflected as she'd revealed the elaborate meal she had wheeled in on a super-sized trolley.

Cordelia had tossed and turned, thinking about how she was going to handle the forthcoming conversation.

Now, here she was, summoned by the very same shy young girl who had delivered her meal the previous evening and taken through the vast, echoing mansion to a sitting room where a selection of breads, cold meats and cheeses were waiting, on a highly polished sideboard, to be sampled.

The appetite that had deserted her the evening before enthusiastically responded to the tempting spread and she was slapping way too much butter on some sourdough bread when she heard the door behind her being pushed open.

She spun round as though yanked by invisible strings and inhaled sharply at Luca, who was standing by the door, one brown hand resting light on the doorknob.

He looked stunning. When did he ever disappoint on that front? she reflected a little sourly.

On every other front, he had come up short, but when it came to looks, he continued to deliver with a punch.

'Good,' he opened, strolling towards her and looking at her plate with satisfaction, 'you're eating. Better than last night.'

'What are you talking about?' Strings cut, her legs remembered what they were there for and she walked towards the small circular table by the bay window, which overlooked the swathes of grapevines.

It was the most relaxing view she had ever had. The sea, in all its glory, was fascinating and ever changing, roaring with black anger one minute, as flat and as calm as a sheet of glass the next. But this was so still, so perfectly peaceful.

It was a reminder of just why she had always craved escape from the narrow confines of her life. To taste all the different things the world had to offer.

It was unfortunate that her first taste had been offered to her in the way it had.

She looked at him with guarded eyes as he sat opposite her with a plate of breads and cheese. It was a small table. She could reach out and touch him if she wanted.

'Sylviana reported back to me, as duly requested.'

'You're now spying on my eating habits?'

'You're carrying my baby. Everything you do now is of importance to me.' He paused and looked at her, taking everything in. Luca wasn't a fool. He knew he had to tread gently, manoeuvre the situation with the agility and expertise of someone navigating a minefield.

She wasn't like any other woman he had ever known. She was like quicksilver. Money didn't interest her, which was something he had found incredibly appealing and frankly still did, it would seem. She had laughed off his marriage proposal because love wasn't on the table. Cold logic dictated that he pay close attention to that line of reasoning. Women always wanted more than he was prepared to give on the emotional front and, even though she had made it perfectly clear that she had never seen them as anything other than a couple of people who'd had a bit of fun, an enjoyable no-strings fling that had escalated into the unthinkable because of the pregnancy...who knew...?

Was the silent rider to his proposal that she would

accept if there was a courtship involved? Did she think that the only way for them to have a permanent relationship would be if they aimed for the fairy-tale ending where he looked soulfully into her eyes and promised her the earth? Did she secretly crave what every other woman craved, aside from Isabella, which was what had made her so suitable a marriage prospect? That gradual breaking down of all defences until you were left as raw, vulnerable and exposed as a mollusc without its shell?

It wasn't going to happen and Luca knew that he had to work his way carefully around that while still getting her on board with the marriage idea, because married they were going to be.

His eyes lingered for a few seconds on her and he found himself staring.

That face of hers. Strong-boned, free of make-up, healthy and without artifice. Her hair was plaited. Just the one plait, which she had dragged over her shoulder. The vibrancy of her blonde hair stood out even more over here in a country where most of the women were brunettes.

He felt his pulse pick up speed and a dragging in his groin. He'd spent the night thinking of her, working out a future that he hadn't bargained for. He'd thought of her and had felt the same ache, reminding him that his libido was all present and intact and had not been sated since he had last slept with the woman now carefully working her way through the various fresh breads she had taken. He'd had a lot on his plate workwise and, with Isabella looming on the horizon, he had not been tempted to immerse himself in any kind of dating scene.

Marriage, he reflected, was not going to be all bad. They would naturally share a bed and, while love in all its nauseating complications wouldn't be part of the equation, sex most definitely was going to be on the menu, and the menu looked very tempting from where he was sitting.

But, he reminded himself with baffled frustration, nothing was going to be on any agenda until vows had been exchanged. Right now, he would do well to keep her at arm's length until the details had been sorted.

'I have already apprised my father of the situation.'

Cordelia looked at him in consternation. 'He must have been devastated. All those plans made...' The enormity of what Luca was prepared to sacrifice for her made her suddenly uncomfortable with her stubborn refusal to play ball. Her head was pointing her in one direction but her heart...what it wanted...

'Have you decided when you will tell your father?'

Cordelia shifted uneasily. Would a simple *'No'* sound too abrupt? It was so complicated, but then she thought of arrangements made from birth, a marriage understood, a future planned, the twinning of great fortunes and everything that came with that... all gone in a whoosh. For Luca, there would be devastation all round and not just for him, but for everyone associated with a marriage that would now never happen.

To his credit, he hadn't raged and stormed and if he'd used the vocabulary of shock, then who could blame him? He certainly didn't seem to be dwelling on the downsides of the situation and she could only reluctantly admire him for that.

'I plan on phoning him later...' she said vaguely.

'But you're not sure.'

'He needs to find out, of course he does.'

Luca sat back and looked at her thoughtfully, gauging the atmosphere, his antennae picking up on things that weren't being said, sensing her doubts and confusion and sympathetically understanding the reason behind them.

She was an innocent. She didn't have the tools at her disposal to deal with some of the things life decided to throw at you. He did. He knew the value of working with what couldn't be changed and then adding the upsides to the situation. It was the difference between winners and losers and he had always been a winner.

He winced. Unlike his father, who had actually congratulated him on living life properly for the first time.

'You have enough money for a thousand lifetimes,' Giovanni Baresi had bellowed down the phone, drowning out the disturbing sound of music and laughter in the background. 'Time you started really finding out what life's all about!'

That had been before he could tell his father that it wasn't the exalted love affair he seemed to believe it was, but an honest mistake that carried consequences. After that bracing, booming, slap-on-the-back response, Luca had held his tongue, and the weird thing was that there was a part of him that had been secretly pleased to have heard genuine admiration in his father's voice.

He had made more money for the family than could be counted in gold coins...he was respected and held in awe by financiers the world over...and yet, telling his dad that he had had a three-week fling with a girl in Cornwall, had got her pregnant and was going to marry her, had elicited more joy and pride than anything he had ever done in his life before.

'I want us to be married,' Luca began with rough sincerity. 'You think it's because I'm a dinosaur. You think I'm mired in pointless tradition that's past its sell-by date because who needs marriage these days when a baby is involved? There are countless single mothers bringing up kids while fathers get a look-in now and again before moving on to have their own families.'

He paused and Cordelia looked at him as his words sank in. Single mothers. Visiting fathers. And then, naturally, those visiting fathers would move on to perhaps have another family. She thought of Luca having children with another woman, Isabella. Children who would be born to roam on these vast estates while on the other side of the ocean...

Her heartbeat sped up and she gulped.

'And maybe,' he continued quietly, 'I *am* a little old-fashioned when it comes to family. Maybe it's beyond the pale to see duty and responsibility as things to be worn proudly on one's shoulders. Yes, I have sometimes yearned to be free to do whatever I want to do but, mostly, I have been content and proud of my heritage and my legacy. Is that a bad thing?'

Luca allowed the rhetorical question to hover in the silence between them.

'I will love our child with everything in me. I will protect him from every sling of every arrow and he, I feel, will learn to love his inheritance the way I have. You tell me that you can't consider marriage without love. Love you may not have, but respect you will, and in abundance.'

But he would never love her. He had just confirmed that, in case she started getting any ideas. She could see the way his brain was working. But was the search for love, if it ever happened anyway, enough to compensate for their child being torn apart from a father who dearly wanted him?

And what about *her* feelings for Luca? They ran deep. Deeper than he could ever imagine and it was no use pretending otherwise. Who would catch her when she was falling hard for a guy who wasn't going to be truly emotionally available to her? The balancing act between her head and her heart made her dizzy.

'And think of that one thing you've always wanted, Cordelia. To see the world. That would be what our child would have were we to marry. There would be no corner of the globe left unexplored. Great wealth, I'm driven to say, can buy travel to the four corners of the world...'

'I... I'll think about it,' Cordelia said helplessly, knowing that he had struck below the belt but unable to resist the glorious image of planes and ships and foreign lands and her child—*their* child—being exposed to all the adventure that went along with that, adventures she had never had.

'Say yes,' Luca urged, leaning forward and taking her fingers in his hand, an absent gesture that made her skin tingle with forbidden pleasure.

'But surely you would eventually resent me? Resent the fact that I had stopped you from marrying Isabella?'

'You haven't stopped me from doing anything,' Luca murmured. 'This decision is my choice. How could I resent you, that being the case? Say yes and here is what will happen next. I will tell Isabella and her family. Tomorrow. And then we will get your father over, tell him face to face. Together. But not just yet. In the meanwhile, I will show you my land, show you my country, show you…what our child will enjoy. What do you say, *mi tesoro*?'

Caught on the horns of a dilemma, she breathed in deeply and sank into the earnest intent in his eyes.

'Okay. I'll say yes—even though…'

'Shh.' He placed his finger over her mouth. 'Yes is enough. No need to qualify it.'

CHAPTER SEVEN

THE FOLLOWING DAY Luca had had his chauffeur drive him the lengthy three-hour round trip to Isabella's parents, where he'd presented the situation as a *fait accompli*, no questions asked, no room for manoeuvre.

He had sat in a living room as grand and as formal as his own, where he had been served delicate morsels and strong coffee in china cups and watched his hosts' disappointment as he'd broken the news. There had been no formal engagement but, between families, the unspoken understanding had been almost as strong, and, while they had politely congratulated him on a marriage no one had foreseen, they could scarcely contain the fact that they had been badly let down.

'It would have been so good for Isabella,' Maria, her mother, had said, shooting a glance at her husband, who had looked away. 'She…'

'Maria!' Alberto had said sharply. 'We do not need to trouble Luca with our regrets. It is as it is.

Naturally, we will continue to work harmoniously together. Our great wines benefit from this close relationship, not to mention the other avenues for development that are in the making.' At which point he had ushered Luca to the cellar where he had shown him his addition of rare reds to the collection he already had.

Both Maria and Alberto were far too well bred to show any emotion and neither had he. It was as it was.

He was more concerned about Isabella. This marriage would have suited her but maybe, he'd thought, on his way back to his villa, it was fate. Perhaps she needed to find the courage to tell her parents about her sexuality instead of trying to hide behind a façade of a happy marriage.

He had, in fact, spoken to Isabella at length on the telephone on the way to her parents'. A face-to-face meeting was out of the question as she was holidaying with friends on the Riviera. He had smiled wryly at the relief in her voice when he had broken the news of his upcoming marriage to Cordelia. Let off the hook for the time being. Her congratulations had been sincere and heartfelt and when he had hung up, it had flashed through his head that neither Isabella nor Cordelia were what might be considered orthodox candidates for walking up the aisle.

One was relieved not to be doing so and the other was doing so only because all alternative exits had been barred. Money, it had to be said, definitely didn't buy love. Just as well, considering it wasn't something he was looking for.

That job over, here he was now, at ten the following morning, waiting at a chic café in the stunning city of Siena. He'd returned late the previous night to find Cordelia dead to the world in one of the guest bedrooms. He had left orders for her to be given whatever she wanted for breakfast and, at a little after six in the morning, he had taken himself off to his head office, where he had powered through key emails and filled various CEOs in on what might prove a temporarily disjointed work schedule.

A makeover for his reluctant wife-to-be was on the cards.

Then, once they were back at his house, a jeweller would be personally escorted on Luca's private plane so that a ring could be chosen.

She had taken some persuading to agree to marry him and he wasn't going to sit on his hands and hope she didn't change her mind. Speed was of the essence and he intended to put his foot on the accelerator until she was bound to him, with all i's dotted and t's crossed.

Woolly nonsense about love not being on the agenda was not going to be a spoke in any revolving wheels.

His father had offered to return to Tuscany immediately so that he could meet the lucky bride and

Luca had only just managed to dissuade him, pointing out that it would be far better to wait a couple of weeks until she was fully settled before bombarding her with yet more stuff to confuse her.

'She's from another...er...' Luca had thought of her, her sinewy, purposeful body, her lightly freckled face bare of make-up, her hair hanging down her back in a riot of tangled curls, and the word *planet* had sprung to mind.

However, any such description wasn't going to do, he'd acknowledged, because his father truly thought that at long last his hard-nosed son had traded his head for his heart, and Luca had been strangely reluctant to disillusion him on that front.

'It's like me and your mother,' Giovanni Baresi had murmured in a trembling, emotional voice down the end of the phone line. 'Same part of the world, even. Oh, my dear, dear son...'

Luca had found it astonishing that, after the many conversations they had had over the years on the subject of relationships and Luca's outspoken disapproval of his father's antics, his father could still be swept away on a tide of emotion at the unrealistic assumption that his son had somehow managed to dispatch his brain on a long-distance holiday, leaving him vulnerable to the one thing he had always declared he didn't believe in.

Having allowed his father to think the wildly improbable, he had had to go with the flow. Likewise, for better or for worse, Isabella and her parents also nurtured thoughts of a love match. Isabella should have known better, considering they had discussed the suitability of a marriage of convenience, but there you had it.

Luca sighed and glanced at his watch.

Who believed what didn't matter anyway, so dwelling on it was a waste of time.

She was late.

He dialled her number and opened, without hesitation, 'Where are you?'

'I'm sorry,' Cordelia responded breathlessly. Sitting in the back seat of Luca's plush four-wheel drive, she could barely take in the splendid sights bypassing them as his driver whizzed along the deserted roads. Her head was moving left to right, her senses darting frantically so that she didn't miss a thing. 'I'm afraid I asked your driver to pull over a couple of times…well, maybe more than a couple, actually…'

'You were sick? Is there a problem?' Luca jerked into an upright position and wondered whether to video call her instead of talking down the end of a phone. So much more could be deciphered from looking at someone and Cordelia was certainly one of those people whose faces were as transparent as a sheet of glass. She wasn't the complaining sort but was there some kind of medical problem happening? He wondered how fast he could get his consultant over to his house.

'Oh, no,' Cordelia responded airily. 'It's just that the scenery is so breathtaking that I wanted to take some pics on my phone.'

Luca sagged with relief, then he clicked his tongue impatiently.

'My PA has set up appointments with the couturier,' he drawled.

'You never said.'

'I didn't think you would waste time stopping on the way for Kodak moments.'

'I still don't understand why I have to…have a change of wardrobe, Luca.'

'You're marrying me, *cara*. You will be entering a world that's far removed from the one you have always been accustomed to. It is just a question of assimilation.'

Cordelia didn't say anything. She had made her decision and she knew that he had a point. She could no longer hang around in jeans and tee shirts because she was no longer going to be living the life she had always lived. Close to the sea, barefoot on a beach, interacting with people who built lives around the ocean. She had dreamed of faraway adventure and now she had got what she'd always wanted, but that dream came at a price and it was too late to start quibbling about how high or low that price should be.

At least when she had earlier spoken to her dad, he hadn't sounded as anxious as she'd expected.

Lord knew, his anxiety levels would shoot through

the roof when she broke the news to him about the pregnancy, but that was a bridge she was happy to cross a bit later.

She could only hope that Doris would keep quiet, but there was nothing she could do about that.

She resisted the urge to make Luca's driver stop again when they entered the city because it was so unimaginably beautiful.

The colours of sand and taupe, buildings that seemed to be carved from the earth, ornate, majestic and breathing an ancient history.

It felt as though, literally, she was entering a different world. She wanted to hop out of the car and begin exploring immediately. Instead, she poked her head through the window and tried hard to take it all in.

Regrettably, they were at the designated meeting spot all too soon for Cordelia's liking.

She tipped into the most amazing open space, a fan-shaped central square ringed by ancient medieval buildings with the occasional modern shop front as a token nod to the twenty-first century. A thin bell tower dominated the vast circle of old buildings and she took a few seconds out to gaze at it.

Luca was sitting outside the café, the name of which he had texted her. He was lounging back in a pair of grey chinos, a white short-sleeved linen shirt and dark designer sunglasses that inconveniently concealed his expression as she walked towards him.

He looked the very essence of sophisticated and laid-back, with an elegance that only money could buy.

No wonder he wanted her out of her uniform of jeans as fast as possible, she thought. He might have found that charming in Cornwall but it was definitely off limits here in his rich life and all that that rich life entailed.

She had a twinge of doubt. Was this really her? She had agreed to marry a guy who didn't love her. She had signed up to a life the rules of which she didn't know. Then she thought of the baby inside her and swallowed back all her fears and misgivings. She had to settle in one camp and put the pull-push feelings away. She also had to stop hoping for the impossible.

Their marriage might not be what she had had in mind for herself but, then again, neither had she ever contemplated the prospect of a pregnancy she hadn't planned and, while Luca might not love her, he had been prepared to sacrifice the direction of his own life to accommodate a situation that would have hit him as hard as it had hit her. That spoke volumes. That was enough because it would have to be enough.

She just couldn't deny their baby the huge advantages of inheriting a lineage that was rightfully his.

Step one would be to accept the path she had chosen without fuss. She wouldn't argue about everything and she wouldn't look further than what Luca could put on the table. She would also stop thinking about the woman he had walked away from, speculating on what he might or might not have felt for her, on what she might or might not look like.

Her future was starting this very moment and glancing over her shoulder wasn't going to do.

'You worried me when you told me that you'd asked Roberto to stop on the way here,' he opened, getting down to business straight away but unable to overlook the tug at his groin when he looked at her. Luca had never had a problem when it came to women and moving on, and he absently wondered whether the fact that she was pregnant with his child somehow accounted for the ongoing effect she seemed to be having on him.

'I'm sorry,' Cordelia parried stiffly as she sat on the chair next to him and facing out onto the square, which was great because it meant she didn't have to look at him, which was a disaster zone for her when it came to thinking clearly. 'I couldn't resist. I've never travelled abroad. It was all too much.' That admission of just how wildly different their worlds were brought a tinge of colour to her cheeks. 'If we're going to be late for…for whatever it is that you've arranged, then perhaps we should leave now.'

'They'll wait.' Luca shrugged. 'I thought all women enjoyed shopping and having things bought for them. You're acting as though I'm punishing you by getting you a new wardrobe. Whatever you want. You name it and it's yours.'

'We're so different, you and I,' Cordelia couldn't help but murmur, glancing across at him and then finding her gaze helplessly locked to his sharp, aristocratic profile.

'We are,' he agreed without hesitation. 'You're not going to start using our differences to return to the discussion about love and marriage, are you?'

'Of course not.'

'Good.' He removed the sunglasses to dangle them on one finger and glanced sideways at her.

So different.

Yet she had taken the plunge and was about to enter a world she would never have envisaged for herself. She would be buffed, polished and primed for life in the luxury lane and he felt that she might be scared stiff at that unknown future ahead of her. It was one thing to talk about exploring different shores. It was quite different when you found yourself dumped on one of those shores with the signposts all in a foreign language, far from everything that might feel familiar.

'This is going to work,' he told her firmly, voice low, waving aside a hovering waiter and standing because there was a lot to do.

'You can't say that.'

'Of course I can. I intend to be an excellent father and an excellent husband.'

'You don't love me.'

Luca cupped her elbow so that he could usher her into the square, away from the café and towards a corner in which was nestled an array of high-end shops, all peeking out from their grand façades of weathered, ochre-coloured brick.

'I will, however, respect you as the mother of my child. Likewise, you will find me a faithful husband.'

Looking at him, Cordelia sighed at the confident, cocky smile he shot her. God, he was so different from her yet he got to her in ways no one else could.

'That's another sweeping statement,' she murmured, although she couldn't help but breathe a sigh of relief that some of her darkest doubts were being addressed.

Not love, but fidelity. It was an exchange that would have to do. Many unhappy relationships ended up with far less.

'I've never approved of my father's search for love,' Luca confessed as they strolled towards the small but exquisite boutique with which he was vaguely familiar. 'He loved once and when that was prematurely ripped away from him, he thought that he could replace it. Love was always just round the corner. Marriage always followed and heartbreak was always the eventual outcome. Not to mention vast drops in the family coffers thanks to greedy exes and expensive lawyers. A wise man can avoid all of that nonsense by making sure he doesn't start picturing a life of happy-ever-afters. So if I'm cynical about the therapeutic powers of love, then I have every reason to be so. That said...' He paused and looked at her with a frown. He was still dangling the sunglasses but now he stuck them on and she shielded her eyes from the bright glare of the sun.

'That said...?' Cordelia prompted.

'That said,' he drawled, shaking himself free from whatever weird hold she'd temporarily exercised on him with those gently questioning, impossibly blue eyes, 'he was always a great believer in the value of monogamy.'

'That's important.' Cordelia fell into step with him as he moved off, heading towards the far corner of the *piazza*.

Luca laughed under his breath. 'His values were always in the right place. It was his heart that couldn't stop hiving off in all sorts of undesirable directions. We're here. Clothes and whatever else you might see that takes your fancy. You'll need everything from shoes to bags to jewellery. Then my PA has arranged for you to hit one of the beauty salons around here. I have the address.'

'It's a comprehensive overhaul.' Cordelia valiantly tried to laugh that off rather than see it as some kind of implied insult.

'You'll thank me for it in the long run. I have an important charity gala to attend in a couple of weeks and you will be on my arm as my wife-to-be.'

Sudden nerves plucked at Cordelia's tummy and she spun round to stride in front of him, stopping him from marching onwards by dint of placing her hand on his chest.

'Why am I only hearing about this now?'

'Does it matter?'

'Luca, I have no experience when it comes to… to that kind of thing…'

'What kind of thing?'

'I don't even know what a charity gala entails!'

'Lots of important people meeting up to have fun while raising money for one or more designated charities. The women will all be dressed to the nines, hence one of the reasons for this shopping trip taking place today.'

'I'm never going to fit in!'

'Don't be negative, Cordelia. You have a fortnight to get used to the idea. These things may be tedious but we're not talking about water torture.'

'The closest I've come to anything like that in my life before,' she protested in a high-pitched voice, 'were the monthly do's at the village hall! I'm thinking that a charity gala isn't going to be in the same league.'

'I would never have taken you for someone so lacking in confidence.'

'I feel out of my depth.'

Luca paused, hitched his sunglasses to the top of his head and looked at her so seriously and so intently that Cordelia could feel hot colour race into her cheeks.

Now he's seeing what he's let himself in for, she thought miserably. *I'm just an ordinary girl from a Cornish village and no amount of fancy dress can ever change that. Is this the point when he decides that marriage might not be such a great idea after all?*

She was astonished at the gaping hole that opened up inside her at the prospect.

It was one thing for him to hitch his wagon to the mother of his child, but quite another to hitch it to a woman who could never possibly live up to his exalted lifestyle.

She stared down at the wildly unfashionable sandals she had brought over with her and started when she felt the graze of his finger against her burning cheek.

'Don't worry,' Luca murmured. He tilted her chin upwards and their eyes met and held. 'You can lean on me. I have no intention of letting you flounder.'

Cordelia blinked.

Every straining muscle in her body was propelling her forward, one small step then another.

She was barely aware of herself leaning up or of her mouth parting, inviting more than just a casual touch.

She closed her eyes and sighed with pleasure as Luca's mouth descended.

* * *

What was going on here? Luca despised public displays of affection. Since when did he do stuff like this? But he was in the grip of something far more powerful than common sense and he plundered her mouth with scant regard for who might or might not be watching.

It was the least cool thing he had ever done in his life before.

But the feel of her lips, her darting tongue, the soft shudder of her body so close to his...

Irresistible.

He drew apart with reluctance and stared down at her.

'We...have things to do...' He raked his fingers through his hair and shifted restlessly. The only thing he wanted to do was grab her hand, head for his car, which was parked less than ten minutes away, and take her back to his house and straight into his bed. 'Clothes to buy,' he muttered thickly.

'My makeover. I know. Sorry. I got...' She couldn't keep looking at him because she would just want to kiss him again. 'I got a little carried away...'

'I think that getting a little carried away is allowed.' He held her hand, linking his fingers through hers in a gesture that felt strangely intimate. 'After all...' he smiled raggedly '...it's not as though we aren't in the most intimate place two people could be in. Yes, getting a little carried away...' he breathed deeply, getting a grip '…is definitely allowed, don't you think?'

Sex, Cordelia thought pragmatically. That was what it was about. That chemistry between them was still alive and kicking and it wasn't all on her side. He wanted her as much as she wanted him. She had felt it in that kiss.

There would be passion and he would be faithful and he would protect her from the slings and arrows of this new life she had to get used to. He'd made that pledge and somewhere deep inside she believed him.

And if there was no love, then three out of four would be good enough.

As he had predicted, they were welcomed into the wonderfully air-conditioned boutique like royalty. The *closed* sign was put on the door and she was invited to take a seat so that clothes could be brought out for her inspection.

She was downright intimidated by the cool grey walls, the marble floor, the clothes hanging on the rails. There was no comforting pop music in the background. Choosing these clothes was serious business. There weren't thousands of items on each rail but she figured that each one would cost a small fortune. It was a minimalist, coldly clinical boutique that only opened its doors to the uber-rich.

She had never felt more uncomfortable in her life before.

A model of similar height but remarkably skinny,

with long dark hair and sultry dark eyes, paraded a selection of outfits while Cordelia sat and tried hard to look riveted by the experience. Ever so often, she murmured and nodded, very much aware of Luca next to her, sprawled on the white leather sofa with his laptop to one side, flickering and demanding attention.

'Okay,' he announced, 'I think we've seen enough.'

The sultry-eyed, dark-haired model looked visibly disappointed at this pronouncement.

Cordelia had scrambled to choose a few things and was already dreading step number two in the makeover. Did she really want to be buffed and polished?

'We'll take…the red dress, the long one and…' he carelessly pointed to the pile that had been set aside to be reviewed '…that lot.' Then he stood up and held out his hand to her.

'You don't have to come with me to the beauty place,' Cordelia said as soon as they'd left the cool boutique and stepped out into the baking summer air.

'I've decided you don't need the spa experience after all.'

'What? Why? I thought I had to have a complete makeover before I could be let loose into high Italian society.'

Luca flushed because, put like that, it didn't seem to say much about him and his values.

Since when had he ever cared what other people thought? He'd been protecting her, but watching that catwalk model parade those clothes had made him realise that she didn't need protecting, at least not when it came to whether she would fit into his world or not.

Naïve and ingenuous she might be, but on the looks front she was head and shoulders above all those women who looked exactly like the dark-haired model. He would guide her through the labyrinth of all those tedious social niceties he had grown up with but, for the rest, she could more than hold her own.

And besides…

It had surprised him to find that he didn't like the thought of her dolled up in all those designer outfits that had been on show.

He was positively turned off at the thought of her in extravagant black outfits or small, intricate dresses that showed off everything and screamed *haute couture*.

'I made a mistake,' he muttered gruffly. He reached for her hand and they began walking away from the stunning *piazza* down one of the many streets that fanned outwards from the main circle.

The impressive architecture didn't stop in the *piazza*. It continued down the side roads—ornate and magical. Legend had it Siena was a city founded by Senius, the son of Remus who was suckled, along with Romulus, by a she-wolf—hence its emblem.

Cordelia had managed to look up some historical facts on the drive and had lapped them up thirstily.

She would have loved nothing better than to have played tourist and seen all the sights but there would be time for that in the future and, for the moment, she was too intrigued by Luca's change of mind to start talking about city tours.

Also, her hand was tingling where their fingers were entwined.

That kiss had lodged in her head and she wanted more. *Man and wife...*

How could she ever have imagined that the chemistry between them wouldn't supercharge given the circumstances? He hadn't looked back when he'd left after those heady three weeks. He had had his life neatly packaged but now here she was and if this was called making the best of a bad deal, then she was going to take it, because she wanted him more than she could ever think of wanting anyone.

'What do you mean?' They were at the car and she stood with her hand on the door, looking at him across the width of the Lamborghini. It was black, sleek and just the sort of high-powered sexy car that needed an alpha male like Luca at the wheel.

'Maybe,' Luca drawled, watching her with his head tilted to one side, 'you awakened a taste in me for everything that's natural.'

'Because I live half my life barefoot and don't own

any make-up?' But her heart was leaping all over the place because that sounded a lot like a compliment.

'Who would have thought that shoes could end up being a highly overrated commodity?' He grinned and raised his eyebrows and she shivered with a sexual awareness that made the hairs on the back of her neck stand on end. 'Besides,' he continued in a lazy drawl, 'I couldn't stand the thought of hanging around in Siena any longer.'

'It's a bore for you,' she agreed, glancing down and then slipping into the passenger seat of the car. It smelled of soft leather. 'I guess you probably thought that it was a waste of time, especially when you probably have lots of work to do.' She turned to him with apologetic eyes because caretaking her really had to be the last thing in the world a guy like him needed or wanted. He was used to expensive women who didn't need to be escorted to the right shops to buy appropriate clothing.

Although hadn't he just said that he liked the thought of her *au naturel…*?

A rush of pleasure surged through her body.

'It would have been a bore for me,' Luca murmured, swivelling so that he was looking at her. He carelessly had one hand by her headrest and he lightly stroked her hair, running one lazy finger through its vibrant blonde curls, 'because I could have thought of a million better things I would rather have been doing with my time.' He paused and then traced her mouth with his finger, tugging on her fuller lower lip until she wanted to faint. 'No, I tell a lie. I would have been thinking of just the one thing I would rather have been doing with my time...'

'What's that?'

Luca laughed, amused. 'Will it turn you on if I spell it out?' He looked at her with satisfaction when she nodded. 'I won't spell it out. I'll show you just as soon as I get you into my bed...'

CHAPTER EIGHT

CORDELIA STRETCHED OUT on the bed and sighed with contentment.

The past week had been a whirlwind. Much of it had been spent in bed, the rest on a voyage of discovery. The day after their visit to Siena, Luca had announced that he intended to keep to his word and show her a bit of his country before she broke the news to her father.

There was work he had to do in Milan, some deals that needed fine tuning. He would arrange for a guide to take her on a personal tour of the city and then they would drive to his house on Lake Como, so that she could see a different countryside from the one she had glimpsed in his Tuscan home.

Vineyards, of course, but also olive trees, oleanders and palm trees and, along with that, incomparable stretches of exquisite villas, their gardens dipping down to the lake shores.

'Italian aristocracy at its very best,' he had wryly

informed her, and when she had asked him whether his house might be amongst those villas, he had laughed and returned, 'But of course. Would you expect otherwise?'

His tone had been one of amused irony but, actually, Cordelia had thought that, no, she wouldn't have expected otherwise. The more she glimpsed of his eye-wateringly privileged life, the more she acknowledged the gaping differences between them.

She was forever telling herself that if he could shrug off those differences, then so would she.

'I want you to feel a little more at home in my country before your father gets here,' he had confided as they had boarded his private jet that would take them to Milan. 'I want you to show him that this is a country that you can love, as I love it. I would not want him to leave with any...doubts that you are doing the right thing.'

Still warm after a bout of passionate lovemaking, Cordelia had thought that that was the nicest thing Luca could have said because it showed that, beyond the baby, he was also thinking about her and her well-being. That counted for a lot.

Milan had been a wondrous place. For someone who had never been abroad, it was mesmerising. Busy but small, it had offered a variety of riches and Cordelia had paid close attention to the charming young guide who had taken her on her whirlwind tour of the city, starting with Piazza del Duomo with its towering cathedral, followed by a visit to see the paintings of the old masters, all of whom were familiar to Cordelia via the many books she had devoured over her lifetime.

This wasn't like Siena with its feeling of medieval splendour and laid-back charm. This was hectic and busy. There were chic cafés everywhere, dotted in between the historic splendour of the *piazza*. The young people all seemed ridiculously good-looking.

She had enjoyed every minute of it and now here she was, enjoying every second of a completely different environment.

From the window of Luca's fabulous villa, she could see the placid waters of the lake in the distance. When the car had first swerved onto the long drive leading to the villa, Cordelia had been gobsmacked. She hadn't bothered to hide her awe. The square white building with its evenly spaced rectangular windows and its formidable symmetry reeked of opulence. From the front of the villa, gardens led down to an archway that opened out onto the lake via a series of shallow stone steps. It was, put simply, breathtaking.

That, however, was a sight that had been taken in several days ago and now, lying here in bed while Luca showered in the fabulous en-suite bathroom, Cordelia could only marvel at the speed with which she was becoming accustomed to this extraordinary life.

'Penny for them.'

Cordelia's eyes shot to the bathroom door where Luca was lounging against the doorframe with a towel slung round his waist. They had already made love that morning and yet she could already feel herself getting turned on all over again. One look at him and stuff inside her ignited and exploded, leaving her wet and weak and at the mercy of his clever mouth and hands and fingers.

'I was just looking out of the window and thinking how beautiful this all is,' she confessed truthfully, watching as he moved from doorway to wardrobe to extract a white linen shirt and a pair of loose trousers, which he dumped over the back of the chair.

Slowly Luca began to dress.

She was, of course, right. It was beautiful, although in truth he rarely noticed the scenery here. In fact, he couldn't think of the last time he had visited this particular property. For Luca, downtime wasn't something he enjoyed very often. The last time, he now mused with some surprise, was when he'd vanished off to Cornwall to get his thoughts together, and look at where that had got him.

A baby on the way and…his eyes roved over the delectable sight of his wife-to-be, pink-faced and tousled, her white-blonde hair spread across the pillow, one long leg draped over the duvet, the other tucked away underneath.

Even when she was relaxing, even when his libido was at rest and sex wasn't on the menu, there was something intensely appealing about her. He was finding that he couldn't keep his hands off, which was just as well considering the situation.

And that situation, he had to admit, was doing very well. He had never, not once, having found out that she was carrying his baby, contemplated not making her his wife. Anything else would have been out of the question, and when she had turned his offer down flat with all that talk about 'love' and 'finding the one' he had momentarily been disconcerted at the notion that she might, actually, walk away from him.

That instant of panic was something he had never experienced before and certainly never in connection with a woman, but she wasn't like anyone else. She was unique insofar as his money was immaterial.

He had appealed to her longing to see the world. It had been, first and foremost, a deliberately well-considered plan to open her eyes to what richness lay in store for her and for their child, and the funny thing was that he had begun to see his own country in a slightly different light.

Had begun to view his own possessions through different spectacles and was appreciating what he had spent a lifetime taking for granted.

He couldn't offer her love, but he could offer her a lot more besides and he could tell that all those bonus extras were weaving their magic.

'This is just the tip of the iceberg,' he murmured, moving to perch next to her at the side of the king-sized bed. 'You have yet to see the splendour of Rome and Florence, although we will try and visit those two cities when there are fewer tourists. Then there is the Riviera...' He couldn't help himself. He drew down the duvet exposing her breasts, bountiful orbs tipped with ripe pink, pouting nipples that begged to be suckled.

'Don't,' Cordelia sighed weakly, relaxing back against the pillow and instinctively arching her naked breast to his mouth. 'We have a lot to do today. Sailing...oh, Luca...oh, yes...' She clasped her hand behind his head as he took her nipple into his mouth and sucked and licked until she was panting and writhing helplessly on the bed.

'The things you do to me,' Luca groaned, vaulting up to strip off the shirt with unsteady hands while his eyes burned into her.

He had work to do. At least a couple of hours before the day could be theirs and yet...he couldn't resist her.

Nor did he intend on shortening the time he had with her, which meant that work would have to take a back seat, which was a first for him and would have been hugely disconcerting if his mind had actually been able to focus on anything other than the woman looking back at him with a helpless yearning that mirrored his.

Their lovemaking was fast and hard and he came

with such intensity that the breath left his body for a few wild moments.

It took him a while to come down from the high. Goodbye any work at all, he thought. Emails would have to be handled later. At some point.

He lay back and flung one arm over his eyes and Cordelia wriggled against him. Warmth spread through her at the feel of his arm heavy across her back and shoulders.

His body was slick with perspiration and she flattened the palm of her hand on his chest.

She loved him. It was as simple as that and the realisation barely shook her because it was something that had crept up slowly but surely, sinking into her consciousness until it was just a fact of life.

She was in love with this guy and that was why she had agreed to marry him. Or at least, it had been a very strong motive, underneath all the very logical reasons she had told herself.

If she had truly felt nothing for Luca but bone-deep indifference, then she would have walked away. Yes, she would have made sure contact was maintained for the sake of their child, but she could never have borne living with someone she didn't care about.

Curiosity and recklessness had propelled her into doing something she would never have dreamt possible given all the principles she had always lived by and, bit by bit over those three weeks, she had fallen for him and fallen hard.

The past week and a half had only made that love deeper, because she had seen him for the good guy that he was underneath the power and the wealth.

All this time he'd taken to show her around, to introduce her to his beautiful country. There was no need for him to have done that!

Surely that meant something?

He was no longer the flint-eyed stranger who had made her want to disappear into the ground when she had first shown up in his office.

She had caught him on the hop, crashed slap bang straight through all the plans he had made for himself, and of course he had been knocked for six, but he had recovered and she wondered whether he wasn't now finding himself at the mercy of feelings he couldn't really express. He gave every semblance of enjoying her company. He was tender and considerate with her, making sure she ate all the right stuff at all the right times. He was the guy she had rescued from the stormy ocean...the guy with no background, no past and certainly no vast fortune to his name.

And they were lovers once again.

Passion was a powerful force and, accompanied by genuine affection...well, how far were those things from love? Not very. There was no point to viewing the future with anything but optimism and, right now, Cordelia was happy to put on rose-tinted spectacles that made the world look so much better.

She snuggled and closed her eyes and enjoyed his nakedness against her.

'Sailing,' Luca murmured drowsily into her hair. 'It awaits us.'

'I thought you were going to try and get through some work before we left…' She ran her fingers along his chest and felt him shudder in instant response, before he absently covered her hand with his. 'You wanted to nail your guy about that project with the refined olive oil…you said he seemed to be digging his heels in on the quality-check front and you were going to push him where you wanted him to be…'

Luca frowned. He must have told her about Giuseppe without even thinking about it.

Disturbed for some reason, he edged off the bed and headed for the shower.

He was gone for a handful of minutes and when he re-entered the bedroom, he was all brisk business as he got dressed.

'You shouldn't have reminded me, *amore*.' He was concentrating on his mobile, only looking up to glance quickly in her direction with his hand on the doorknob. 'Now I'll have to deal with him or my guilty conscience will get the better of me. The great outdoors might have to be put on hold until tomorrow.' He watched her disappointment with a veiled expression.

This was all going swimmingly but it was fair to say that disappointment was part and parcel of life. He should know. His father, embroiled in his own emotional world, had largely been a bystander in his life. Luca had learned from an early age to expect little from a guy who never attended sports days and had shown scant interest in the personal goings-on of his son. Disappointment, he had long ago concluded, did wonders for developing tough independence.

And she would need it because she would realise soon enough that long days doing nothing were not the norm and weren't going to last for ever.

He frowned and restlessly raked his fingers through his hair, because her attempts at a bright, sympathetic smile were worse than outright annoyance that plans had changed.

'Sure,' she said cheerfully. 'I get it.'

'I will arrange for someone to show you around.'

'No need. I can explore on my own. I might even do a bit of sailing. I could probably give a few courses to the instructors out here. You keep telling me to take it easy but that's not what I'm used to. A little exercise will do me the world of good.' She waited for a light-hearted response, which didn't come so she shuffled off the bed, for some reason self-conscious of her body because of the sudden drop in temperature between them.

Freed to do what Luca knew he did best, namely bury himself at work, which would be a timely reminder this mini break was a means to an end, he found himself hovering and watching her through narrowed eyes as she took herself off to the en-suite bathroom, making sure to lock the door behind her.

'Don't take any risks,' he warned gruffly, as soon as she was back in the bedroom, fully clothed in some khaki shorts and a white tee shirt.

'Risks like what?' She looked at him, perplexed.

'You're pregnant.'

'I know. Go slow.' Cordelia's smile felt forced. Of course she was. It was a simple statement of fact but it felt like cold water being dashed over her. That shift in atmosphere—the sudden need to attend to work... Had Luca sensed something in her? Something tender and vulnerable? Something that wasn't part of the package deal? Had she transmitted feelings to him by osmosis and had he reacted by pulling back the way he had?

It made sense.

'I'm strong. I'll manage and, don't worry, I won't take any risks. I may just have a nice stroll and explore what's around.' The smile broadened and felt more forced. 'What time shall I aim to be back here?'

'I would rather you had a personal escort.'

'And I would rather do my exploring on my own without someone trailing behind me to make sure I don't trip over any paving stones.'

'Why are you suddenly being difficult?'

Tension spiked and, for a second, Cordelia was sorely tempted to come right out and tell him what was on her mind. Was he worried that she might be getting too emotionally involved with him when he'd specifically told her that love wasn't on the menu? Was he afraid that she might start making demands he wouldn't be able to meet?

Fear at where such a conversation might lead gripped her and she backed away from it fast.

'Nothing. I guess I'm just a little disappointed that I'll be spending a whole day without you.'

Luca visibly relaxed. He strolled towards her and smoothed his hand over her arm. She had skin as soft as satin.

'Me too.' He was tempted to dump the work but that wouldn't do. Behaving out of character when he was around her was becoming a career choice and he didn't like it, even though he could rationalise it well enough. She was having his baby so of course he was going to treat her differently! 'I'll meet you mid afternoon. I should have had everything wrapped up by then. Keep your mobile handy and I'll call you. We can have tea.'

Cordelia thought that this was how awkward moments were navigated. Was this a prelude of things to come? Small, emotional inroads always taken under cover? Her love hidden away for fear that if he sensed it, he would back off? There was no point dwelling on it, she decided. She would go and have an enjoyable day. When she smiled this time, it was genuine.

'Sure. No rush. If I don't hear from you, I have the address and I can make my way back. Everything feels pretty close so I'm sure I'll be able to walk where I want to go. See you later!'

She headed for the door and knew that he was following her through the villa to the imposing front door overlooking the lake. She didn't want to do anything silly and tempting like spin round and fling her arms around him because she hated the way things had suddenly and inexplicably gone frosty, but instead she slipped on her boat shoes, glanced over her shoulder without making eye contact and gave a little wave.

She had her map.

She'd spent a lifetime longing to leave the Cornish coastline, to see the world. She was seeing it now and she couldn't afford to live off her nerves, letting her imagination get the better of her and letting all the considerable wonders at her fingertips pass her by.

She would have to obey the rules of the game and if that meant keeping her love hidden away like a shameful secret, then she would do that.

Luca wanted to go to one of the windows to follow her progress to the shore.

Perhaps he had allowed that temporary blip in his good humour to show through, but wasn't the occasional mood allowed? She'd also laughed off his concerns about her safety but, hey, wasn't a little paranoia allowed on his part? She was carrying his child and accidents happened!

Luca was not accustomed to worrying about a woman. He wasn't accustomed to imaginary scenarios about unlikely things that might or might not happen on a simple walk by a lake.

He repeated the mantra about this not being a normal situation because she was the mother of his baby. It worked for a while but when he discovered that he had been staring at the same page of the report he had been reading on his email for fifteen minutes, he was forced to concede that the mantra, while it made sense, wasn't having the desired effect.

Like it or not, his head was crammed with a variety of possible dangers she might encounter because she felt she needed some exercise and fresh air.

He couldn't squash his fears even though there was nowhere on earth safer than the shores of this stunning lake. For a start, there were endless tourists around. It wasn't one of the smaller, quieter lakes. If she slipped or fell or fainted or urgently needed to lie down, there would be people around to help and she'd call him, but none of those things would happen anyway because all she would do was stroll and maybe stop and have something to drink at one of the cafés. You couldn't walk five metres without colliding into a packed café.

Not that she was going to slip. Or fall. Or faint. Or urgently need to lie down.

But what if she did?

He would never forgive himself. Protecting her was his duty. The place for him right now wasn't in front of his computer trying to focus. It was by her side…making sure she didn't slip.

Mind made up, he left his villa at speed. He hadn't been to the villa for a hundred years, or so it seemed, but he knew this lake like the back of his hand. Just one of the many exotic destinations he had frequented in his early days. It was muggy outside. Grey skies and the lake wearing an angry look, as though thinking about getting choppy.

Luca ignored the crowds. How far had she walked? He was approaching at pace by the time he spotted her, laughing on one of the rental boats, of which there were many. This one was a small, sleek, mahogany little number, your basic speed-boat made for two.

And she was with a guy, which made him pull up short.

Blond hair in a ponytail, tanned, wearing a shirt that was stupidly unbuttoned all the way down and surfer shorts.

Something wild and primitive ripped through Luca and he had to take a few seconds to gather himself.

They were laughing.

He thought back to that tight smile she had given him before stalking out of the villa earlier and he saw red. Fists bunched, he breathed in deep and by the time he made it to the boat, he was in control.

'Having fun?'

In the midst of trying to make herself understood, in Italian, to the very pleasant guy from whom she was trying to rent the boat, Cordelia took a few seconds to register that Luca had shown up, far earlier than she had expected.

She turned around and, smile fading as she took in his glowering expression, she tentatively said, 'You're early. I didn't think you'd be here for a couple of hours.'

She was standing on the deck of the small outboard motorboat, and she leapt off with the surety of a gazelle.

She knew boats as well as she knew the changing moods of the ocean.

Shading her eyes with one hand, she turned around and offered a very poor goodbye in Italian to Elias, the young guy who was now not going to get the rental he wanted.

'What are you doing?' Luca enquired coolly, having restrained himself from being just too aggressive for no reason towards a perfect stranger.

'What do you mean?'

'I thought you were going to have a stroll and maybe grab some lunch somewhere. Instead, you've decided that that's all too tame and you'd rather risk life and limb on a speedboat...'

Cordelia's mouth dropped open. 'Luca, there's no need for you to be overprotective! Are you forgetting that I rescued you from the sea? I've been handling boats faster and bigger than this since I was ten.'

'You're pregnant. You shouldn't be thinking of doing anything as reckless as sailing. Of course, if I'm with you, then that's a different story.'

They were heading towards the centre of the village, a charming honeycomb of small winding streets jam-packed with attractive, expensive shops, cafés and restaurants. Tables set out on the pavements were filled with tourists playing people-watching.

Luca veered off the main thoroughfare down one of the smaller avenues and eventually they managed to find themselves a quiet corner in one of the restaurants.

'And who was that boy you were laughing with?' he asked with a scowl.

'Elias?'

Luca nodded and shrugged and looked away for a few seconds before scrutinising the menu and ordering nothing more than a double espresso from the waiter who had sidled up to the table.

'He was the guy in charge of the boat rentals.' Cordelia broke off to order a selection of little cakes, irresistible, before returning her gaze to his face with a frown. 'Why?'

'No reason. Should I have one?'

'I have no idea what you're getting at.' The coffee and the cakes arrived and Cordelia gazed at them, marvelling at how perfectly formed each one was. Almost a shame to eat them. She wasn't looking at Luca at all.

'You seemed a little familiar.'

Her eyes flew to meet his.

'Luca, were you...*jealous*?'

'Jealous?' Luca sat back and drummed the tabletop with his fingers while he looked at her with a brooding expression. 'I have never been jealous in my entire life.' He gestured in a way that was exotically Italian and gave a bark of laughter. 'I don't believe in jealousy. It's a corrosive emotion.'

Cordelia didn't say anything because what he really could have said was that he didn't do jealousy because to be jealous you had to have some kind of intense emotion inside you for someone, and intensity on that level wasn't something he was capable of feeling.

Suddenly deflated, she fiddled with the small fork that had been placed in front of her.

'However,' Luca gritted, 'I'm an old-fashioned man with old-fashioned principles. I don't care for the idea of my woman flirting with other men.'

At that, she met his steely gaze with a look of outraged incredulity. *His woman?* That level of possessiveness seemed to beg for a far deeper connection than business arrangement for the sake of a baby with someone you had a fling with, but she decided to let it pass. Was it a case of a business arrangement and keeping her at arm's length except when his arrogance kicked in, at which point she turned into *his woman*?

'I wasn't flirting,' she said in a low voice.

'You were laughing.'

'Since when is laughing the same as flirting?'

'It's a damn sight more than I managed to get from you today,' Luca gritted in immediate response.

Uncomfortable with a show of feeling that was so far removed from his usual calm, cool and collected responses to anything that asked for an emotional response, Luca concentrated on drinking his espresso. There was no point continuing a conversation that seemed mired in abstract nonsense.

So what if he'd been jealous? It was only natural. A wife-to-be was quite different from a passing conquest.

Jealousy had never been an issue with Isabella. Perfect.

'A person can't be in a happy mood all the time,' Cordelia pointed out, finishing the last of the tasty delicacies and licking the very last of the icing sugar from her finger while she thought about how he had changed earlier on, gone from light-hearted and warm to suddenly as cold as the Arctic sea. From wanting to spend time with her to needing to spend time on his computer.

'I get that,' Luca growled. When it came to happy moods, he hadn't, after all, written the book. 'But I want you to be. I... I'm going the extra mile... I'm *trying*.'

'What are you talking about?'

Luca didn't want her to feel tempted to return to the life she was going to be leaving behind. Showing her his country was a labour of love, more so because he seemed to be seeing so many beautiful parts of it for the first time himself, but he knew that it was also his way of getting her on board. He didn't see anything devious about that. It seemed perfectly fair and reasonable.

Luca tightened his jaw and reminded himself that, first and foremost, he was a man who never allowed any part of his body to govern his behaviour except for his head.

The feathers that had been stupidly ruffled by that admission of jealousy smoothed back into their normal position and not a second too soon.

'I'm showing you my beautiful country.' He gestured around him but his fabulous eyes remained pinned to her face. 'I am putting work concerns on the back burner so that I can bring you to a place like this!'

'And so I should be smiling all the time?' An unwelcome picture began to form, one that killed off any romantic notions that what he felt for her might, actually, have legs.

She could read between the lines as good as the next person.

He was putting himself out to entertain her and it wasn't because he was necessarily enjoying it or even really wanted to. Everything had changed for Luca the second he had found out that she was carrying his baby and he had rolled with the punches because that was the kind of guy he was.

He had sussed the situation, known the direction he wanted it to go in and had altered his programme accordingly.

Did he think that if he'd handed her over to a tour guide and returned to his work schedule, she might have reconsidered the marriage option?

Had it occurred to him that, as a husband in the making, it wouldn't have done to have given her the wrong impression? She'd turned down his marriage proposal to start with…it made sense for her to have a visible demonstration of what she would be getting if she took him up on the offer after all. He'd won her with his persuasive arguments and maybe he thought that, yes, he would go the extra mile in making sure she didn't change her mind.

'Of course, I appreciate all the hard work that's gone into making me feel welcome,' she concurred coldly, pushing away the flowered plate and sitting back to rest her hands on her lap.

Luca had the grace to flush. 'That is not what I meant.'

'Sounded like it to me.'

He glared and dumped his serviette on the table with a flourish and summoned the waiter to pay the bill.

'Let's move on from this conversation.' He offered his hand to help her and she took it readily enough but then dropped it the second she was on her feet. 'I feel it's one that could end up going round in ever-decreasing circles and getting nowhere fast.'

'Sure.' She was going to have to look at the bigger picture. She was going to have to see this upcoming union for what it was and look for no more than what was on the table.

She would enjoy the last couple of days in this wonderful place because, all too soon, she would have to tell her dad about the pregnancy and break it to him that she would not be returning to Cornwall, but making her home on the other side of the ocean.

'We will be back in Tuscany in no time at all.' Luca mirrored what she was thinking with uncanny accuracy. 'Let's try and relax here. Stress is no good for a pregnancy. There will be much to do when we return.'

So factual, Cordelia thought, so well-mannered, and if she wanted more then that was her problem and nothing to do with him.

CHAPTER NINE

HER FATHER WOULD be coming over for the charity gala.

'It makes sense,' Luca had pointed out in the sort of voice that implied that anyone who didn't agree with that sweeping statement was clinically insane.

'He'll be walking into something he hasn't banked on and he's not the kind of man who would know what a charity gala is.' Cordelia's voice had been laced with scepticism. 'He doesn't even own a suit. Or if he does, it will be the one he was married in and it probably won't fit. And that's the kind of thing he would want me around to help him with. Choosing a suit.' Her eyes had welled up.

'He won't be walking into it unprepared,' Luca had returned equably. 'He has already accepted that you've looked me up over here and he probably suspects that the very reason you left Cornwall in the first place was to get in touch with me. He's already overcome the disappointment that you didn't tell him the truth in the first place. So we tell him that there will be an event taking place. Who knows? He might look forward to it.'

Cordelia had maintained a healthy silence on the matter. What did Luca know? She hadn't cared for his remark about the disappointment her father had had to overcome but she hadn't been able to argue the logic behind the remark. Luca, she had discovered, didn't pull his punches. If something had to be said, then he said it. End of story.

Heaven only knew what her father thought of her now, lying to him about this trip.

There was no way Luca could understand how she was feeling and, even though she didn't want to sound vulnerable and needy, she hadn't been able to stop herself from confiding in him when the plan had been hatched up.

That was how he got to her. One minute her head was telling her to look for nothing, to play it cool, to accept the conditions that had been imposed on this relationship. It was a situation that had been forced on him and there was nothing offensive in the fact that he was rising to the occasion and doing whatever was within his power to make her feel comfortable about the choice she had made. He was proud that he had gone the extra mile. So what right did she have to be upset about it?

She should be able to maintain a stalwart and adult silence on all things personal, but then the second something began weighing on her mind, like the thought of her father coming over to Italy, leaving his beloved Cornwall behind, and being confronted with the sort of over-the-top event he wouldn't know how to cope with, she instinctively turned to Luca to hear what he had to say.

Even though he was the instigator of the whole thing! How did that begin to make sense?

Love, she had thought with helpless desperation.

'Don't underestimate the power of change,' he had advised her in that calm, utterly reasonable voice of his. 'You may find that you've kick-started something you hadn't foreseen. He might have discovered that he can manage just fine without you around. Might prefer it, even.'

Now, with her fancy dress laid out on the bed and a bath run, Cordelia thought back to what Luca had said. There was a knot in her stomach. Her dad would be arriving at Luca's villa in under three hours, before the charity gala was due to begin. He was walking into a rolling estate the likes of which he had never seen before and he would quickly realise the set-up and just how magnificent it was going to be. She had gaily told him that Luca, despite what they had both originally assumed, was pretty well off. She'd played down the extent of his wealth because somehow it seemed okay for 'pretty well off' to be a simple oversight on Luca's part, something that might not have reasonably come up in conversation, whereas, 'billionaire who owned vast vineyards and

half of Italy' wasn't quite such an acceptable oversight. And something in her resisted the thought of
denigrating the guy she was so hopelessly and fool-
ishly in love with.

'You just don't know what you're going on about,'
she announced out of the blue.

Standing in the doorway to the en-suite bathroom
with just his jeans on, because he had discarded his
white linen shirt on the ground, Luca paused and
looked at her with a frown.

There were times when she was so utterly illogical that he was reduced to complete speechlessness.

Who'd have thought? She could swim like a fish
for miles, could handle a boat like a sailor and could
talk to fishermen as if she were one of them, making them obey her orders without complaint, and
yet, out of the blue, she said something like this that
left him scratching his head and wondering what
the hell she was talking about. Unpredictable. He'd
never cared for unpredictable but he'd had to get
used to it and fast.

Whatever she was now trying to say, his gut feeling
told him it was going to be a convoluted conversation.

'Trust me,' Luca said smoothly, deliberately going
for what he knew she wasn't talking about, but seeing it as a safe port in what could be an uncomfortable gathering storm, which was the last thing either
of them needed hours before a gala where their engagement was going to be officially announced to

all and sundry. 'That dress is going to look amazing on you, *tesoro*.'

Cordelia was sufficiently distracted by that random comment to look down at the dress laid out on the bed by the young housekeeper. She'd tried it on the one time a hundred years ago in that shop, forgotten what she looked like in it, and now quailed at the thought of appearing in it in front of a bunch of people she didn't know.

It was long, which was reassuring. But it was tight, which most definitely was not.

And then there were the shoes. Several inches of nude into which her feet would have to be squeezed.

'I'm going to look like a clown,' she muttered.

Luca raked his fingers through his hair and half smiled. This was what he liked, this connection that ran like a current between them. It felt, suddenly, as though a signpost that had been there all along was staring him in the face, pointing him in a direction, and he frowned, in the grip of something he couldn't quite grasp even though, deep inside, he felt that he would be able to if he thought a bit harder about it.

All he knew was that he missed her easy laugh when it wasn't there and the way she would look at him, those slanting glances that always turned him on as no one else had ever been able to. He missed the way he occasionally felt taken for granted and didn't seem to mind all that much. He missed the essence of her, although he wasn't really too sure what that essence was. He just knew that in some low-level way, he missed it.

Hearing the uncertainty in her voice relaxed him now because she sounded more normal, more like the girl he'd so quickly become reacquainted with ever since she had appeared on his doorstep with her bombshell revelation.

'You could never look like a clown.' Luca strolled towards her, a slow smile transforming the harsh contours of his beautiful, lean face.

'I can't tell you the last time I wore a dress.' Annoyingly, Cordelia was finding it hard to hang onto what she had meant to say to him. He was so close now that she could smell the late summer warmth on his skin and see the ripple of muscle in his chest and shoulders. He always knew that the rough edges could be smoothed like this, with a touch.

The second he got just a little too near her, she couldn't seem to help herself. She could be cross, angry, dejected or plain frustrated to within an inch of her life, and her body would still do its own thing, would still curve towards him like a plant turning towards the sun, searching for nourishment.

'What about those dances you tell me you used to go to…?'

'Dances?'

'Where all the local talent would strut their stuff once a month in the village hall.'

'A lot of people found the love of their lives at

those dances,' she pointed out. 'Maybe if I'd worn dresses instead of trousers, I might have been one of the lucky ones.'

Luca lowered his eyes. He didn't say a word and she had a sudden urge to prod him into something more than tactful silence, but what would be the point of that? They were where they were.

'Before you distracted me with the whole dress thing,' she said, although impetus had been lost, 'I was going to tell you that you just don't know anything about Dad.'

Temporarily lost, Luca looked at her with bewilderment. She wasn't going to clarify. She was going to wait until he clocked on with where she was going with this and woe betide if he missed the turning.

He felt something shift inside him, some illogical feeling that made him vaguely uncomfortable even though it was a feeling that he perversely liked.

'You mean,' he said slowly, thinking on his feet, 'the bit about him not being as nervous about being here at the gala this evening as you think he might be?'

'That's exactly what I mean.'

Luca breathed a sigh of relief. He cupped the side of her face with his hand and looked at her solemnly. 'I meant every word of it, *cara mia*. You've clung to one another over the years and I am sure he has built up a dependency on you because of that, has been fearful of you striking out because past experience has taught him that striking out can end in tragedy, but you have cut that tie and don't be surprised to find that he's more resilient than you think he will be. I mean, did he express any hesitation about making the trip over here?'

'Not as such.' She shrugged.

'There you go. Point proven.'

'Because he felt badly about complaining down the end of a telephone doesn't mean that he actually wants to be over here. He's going to be gutted when I tell him…what I have to tell him.'

'We could break the news together,' Luca suggested and she laughed shortly.

'You mean like the happily loved-up couple we're not?' She regretted the words as soon as they left her mouth. She'd made it sound as though this were a black-and-white situation. Her voice had been tart and sarcastic and bitter.

'I'm sorry,' she muttered indistinctly, and Luca looked at her with suddenly cool eyes.

'I don't know what's going on with you, Cordelia, but, whatever it is, you need to put it on hold, at least for the duration of this gala. Do you think you could do that?'

Cordelia wanted the ground to open up and swallow her because what had he done but try and deal with what had landed on his lap in the most gentlemanly way possible? He was right when he said that that had been an unnecessary outburst. More to the point, it wasn't true. He might not be in love with her, but what they had was certainly not the cold, emotionless relationship of two people forced into an arrangement against their will.

They talked, they laughed, they made love and there was sufficient affection there for her to really believe that he would do his utmost to be a good father and a good husband.

'I'm just nervous.' She lowered her eyes, hating the drop in temperature between them. She needed his support and driving a wedge between them just at this moment seemed an incredibly stupid thing to have done.

She took a couple of faltering steps towards him and looked at him hesitantly.

She felt rather than saw some of the icy tension ease out of him and it flashed through her mind that if he could touch her and banish all thoughts from her head, then she could do the same for him.

It was the power of sex and, while it certainly wasn't love, there was something vital and fierce about it and she should be very happy that it was still there, like an electric charge always running between them.

'We'll be late.' Luca raked his fingers through his hair and fidgeted on his feet, suddenly restless.

'I don't know what you're talking about,' Cordelia murmured and he looked at her with a wicked gleam in his eyes.

'I'll bet.' He pulled her towards him. His breathing had thickened and he was already smoothing his hands over her waist, hitching up the shirt and then tugging down the zip of her trousers. 'It's a low trick to use sex to change my mood,' he growled, with rampant amusement in his voice. 'I like it.'

Their lovemaking was fast and hard and mind-blowingly passionate.

By the time they hit the bed, clothes had been scattered on the ground. There was none of the usual foreplay. He kissed her urgently, hungrily, and she was wet and hot when he slid one expert finger into her, stoking her moisture and sending her pulses shooting off in all different directions.

She curled her fingers into his hair and arched back as he drove into her and all it took was one thrust for her to feel the exquisite rising pleasure of a soaring orgasm.

Her groan was long and guttural as her whole body stiffened against his rigid shaft. He came as fast as she did, rearing up and thrusting deeper into her.

'Jesus, woman,' he said in a shaky voice, when they were both back on planet Earth, 'what was that all about?'

'Don't you know?' she breathed.

His head was buried against the nape of her neck and he was limp against her. She stroked his shoulders and was overwhelmed with a feeling of complete tenderness. There were times when he seemed so vulnerable. Times like right now.

'We need to get ready.' His voice was muffled and he tilted his head to one side and their eyes met, a long, steady gaze that made her hold her breath because it felt *loaded*.

He levered himself up and stood, staring down at her. 'Your dad is going to be here in a couple of hours. I don't think he'll be too impressed if he finds us in bed, do you? Although he would have a pretty vivid picture of how we ended up where we have, with a baby on the way.'

With which, he vanished into the bathroom to emerge less than twenty minutes later, giving her plenty of time to get into her finery.

Clothed, Luca was impressive. Naked, he was mind-blowing, but now was certainly not the time to hang around appreciating his masculine athleticism and perfectly toned body.

Sylviana, the young girl who had made her appearance on day one, was going to be helping her get ready and Cordelia didn't wait to watch Luca change.

There was nothing for her to do because an army of hired help had been brought in to prepare the house and grounds for the event. Nothing would be left to chance. From the food to the decorations—everything would be the epitome of perfection.

'It's a well-run machine,' Luca had informed her a couple of days previously. 'Same faces with the only changes being some VIPs I'm hoping to do business with from the Far East and their various assorted family members and professional colleagues.'

The only snag was the fact that his father would not be able to make it because, with first-class ticket in hand and ready to depart from the small Caribbean island where he had ended up after a couple of months of travelling, a world-class hurricane had decided to put paid to his plans.

Privately, Cordelia had been relieved. One father at a time was plenty enough.

Her nerves were all over the place as she got ready. When Sylviana had entered the bedroom, as sweet and as helpful as ever, Cordelia had heard the distant sounds of things happening downstairs, but as soon as the bedroom door was shut, there was complete silence save for their low murmurs as Cordelia dressed.

The redness of the dress was a direct challenge to that tomboy side of her that only ever felt comfortable in jeans, and she hesitated for a few seconds before Sylviana laughed and informed her, in very broken English, that she was going to look beautiful in it.

Really? Cordelia wanted to say. *Even though I'll be the tallest woman there, and that's without the five-inch heels?*

Italian women were dark and dainty and impossibly pretty, she had discovered, and she didn't think that this charity gala was going to prove otherwise.

She didn't glance at herself in the mirror as she got dressed. Sylviana was keen to do the make-up and Cordelia could think of nothing she wanted more because her ability to don warpaint was minimal.

She sat at the dressing table, closed her eyes and let the young housekeeper do her thing.

Her thoughts drifted. There was so much she had to tell her father. She had spoken to him several times on the phone but he was no good when it came to lengthy conversations on the telephone and she, for her part, had felt that there was too much she couldn't tell him for their conversations to be natural and easy.

She hadn't asked how the Doris connection was working out and he hadn't volunteered any information. He'd talked about his catches for the day.

She dreaded to think what would happen when he learned that she, Cordelia, would be spending the majority of her time in Italy. Her brain ached from thinking about it all.

She was on a different planet when Sylviana told her to wake up.

'Is ready, Signorina Cordelia.'

The reflection staring back at her in the mirror was a woman she didn't quite recognise.

The contours of the face were the same, but the subtle application of make-up had given her aristocratic cheekbones and…were her lips really so full… her eyelashes quite so thick and long?

Her curls hadn't been tamed but they *had* been styled to ripple down her back in a far more orderly fashion.

But the most amazing thing was a figure she had always taken for granted.

Tall, rangy, not particularly curvy had been transformed into six feet of elegance once the nude heels were on.

Cordelia turned round and giggled a little nervously as she reached for the gold clutch bag, which was completely empty save for her mobile phone in case her dad called while she was busy bustling downstairs.

She towered over Sylviana but she was still walking on air as she got accustomed to the heels and made her slow way down the staircase in the general direction of the noise.

Vast areas of the house had been transformed and when she glanced outside, she could see that the same applied to the grounds, with tiny lights everywhere, and lanterns hanging from the trees.

When it was completely dark, it would make a marvellous sight.

This was going to be her home. This magnificent, palatial house was going to be where their child grew up. If they stayed together, who knew? There might very well be other children.

They would have all of this at their disposal. The world would be their oyster. When Cordelia thought of the lovely but narrow life she had lived, when she thought back to her yearning to see what was out there, she knew that she had done the right thing in agreeing to marry Luca.

How could she have, in good conscience, denied their child this birthright?

She paused to glance at the frenetic activity in the hall. It would be chaos in most of the other rooms.

Where was Luca?

She didn't think he would be found tasting the food to see whether any further tweaks were needed.

In fact, the thought of him doing that brought a smile to her lips because if there was one thing he had zero interest in, it was what went into the production of all those fine meals that were brought to him by his very talented and loyal staff. Food was always an amusing accompaniment to the main event, which was the wine.

She headed away from the kitchens and the fuss happening in that expansive wing of the villa.

She headed in the direction of his office because she knew that he would probably be working.

It got quieter. She thought of their lovemaking and that, too, made her smile and fired up something proprietorial inside her. He'd made that remark when he had surprised her chatting to the guy with the boat for hire at the lake. *His woman.* There were times when she had a similar feeling, which was that Luca was *her man*.

The office door was ajar when she got there. Where the rest of the sprawling mansion was floored with a mixture of wood and marble, a combination of cool and warm, the long corridor with the far more comfortable rooms leading off it, including Luca's office, was carpeted.

Her steps were soundless. She couldn't hear anything inside but she pushed open the door just to make sure he wasn't there and froze.

Literally, she could feel a coldness washing through her, turning her to ice.

She was numb with it as she looked, open-mouthed, at Luca and the woman in his arms.

They didn't see her. The office was in semi-darkness, as was the corridor down which she had walked, so there was no back light behind her as she watched and stared.

They were standing and they were...entwined. That was the only word for it. Entwined. He had his hands in the woman's hair and Cordelia could hear the sound of quiet, muffled sobbing.

Isabella.

She didn't know how she knew that, she just did. The small, fragile woman curled against Luca was the woman he had been destined to marry, and of course the reason there was so much sobbing going on would be Isabella's distress that she was not going to be the name announced as the lucky fiancée.

She would not be the one flashing the enormous diamond on her finger and accepting congratulations.

What Cordelia was looking at was a love that would never be fulfilled because of her and a pregnancy Luca had never banked on.

She felt sick. She also couldn't move because her feet seemed to have become cemented to the square foot of carpet on which she was standing.

Luca was the first to notice her presence and she saw him still, and his body language must have transmitted something to the woman in his arms because she, likewise, looked up, and now they were both looking at her in complete silence.

'I'm guessing—' at long last she found her voice, and she was pleased that it didn't shake or wobble or worse '—that I've interrupted a special moment between you two?'

'Cordelia…'

Luca's voice was hoarse, emotional in a way she had never heard him be emotional before and, more than anything else, that brought the sting of tears to her eyes.

Isabella was untangling herself from his embrace, making a move to come towards her, and Cordelia, horrified at the prospect of having to listen to some love-struck platitudes, was suddenly galvanised into action.

She began backing away. The high heels were an encumbrance. She wanted to run as fast as she could, but all she could manage was a fast-paced hobble, one hand lifting the long red dress, the other clutching the little bag so tightly she suspected it wouldn't survive the vice-like grip.

She was aware of Luca saying something in Italian behind her but she was oblivious to his approaching steps until she felt his hand circle her arm, pulling her to a stop.

Heart beating like a sledgehammer, Cordelia swung around to look at him and spied Isabella standing hesitantly in the doorway of the office, as dainty and as fragile as spun glass. Her eyes were red from crying but, even so, she remained a beautiful woman, with dark, chocolate-brown hair upswept and a long black dress accentuating a gamine figure. There was a glittering choker at her neck, a string of diamonds that would have cost the earth, befitting the woman who, as Luca had once told her, was his appropriate match.

It was obvious that, along with that understatement of the year, there were a million other things he had failed to mention.

'Cordelia…'

'I don't want to hear, Luca.' Her eyes were dark with disappointment, anger and hurt. 'How could you?'

'How could I *what*?'

'I don't know…' Her voice was laced with biting sarcasm but underneath the acidity she was all too aware of the gathering storm as her mind flew off in all sorts of directions. 'Hmm…let me think…how could you *what*, I wonder? Abandon your own stupid gala so that you could have a final intimate moment with the woman you always wanted to marry? Is that a good beginning to your question, Luca?'

'This is ridiculous.'

'No, Luca…' She tugged at the exquisite diamond on her finger, remembered when it had been chosen and what she had felt when, only a couple of days ago, after it had been sent away for refitting, it had been slipped onto her finger. '*This*…' she handed him the engagement ring '…is ridiculous.'

'I can't believe I'm hearing this. You've got to be joking!'

'Take the ring, Luca, because I don't want it.'

'You're overreacting and interpreting something in completely the wrong way.'

'Am I? I don't think so. Correct me if I'm wrong, but that *was* Isabella, wasn't it? The old family friend you were always destined to settle down with? One wealthy family marrying conveniently into another wealthy family?'

Luca remained silent.

He was put on the spot, all the years of never explaining himself coming to the fore. He clenched his jaw. He wasn't going to take the ring, which was lying in the palm of her outstretched hand. Intense frustration washed over him.

'You're wrong in whatever assumptions you're making, Cordelia. You need to trust me on this.'

His words hovered between them. For a second, Cordelia stopped to consider what he had just said, but only for a second because, as far as she was concerned, if she'd misread the situation, then it was up to him to clarify.

How hard was that? More to the point, was this what marriage to Luca was going to be? What had she agreed to take on? What would be the role of a convenient wife? Exactly?

Part of her wanted to curl her fist round that ring and shove it back on her finger because when she projected to a future without him, she literally quailed with fear.

But a greater part was forced to ask the question— would marriage mean hugging to herself a love that could never be brought out into the open? A love that turned her into someone so emotionally dependent on Luca that it was okay for him to do exactly as he pleased without explanation? Would she be facing a life of having to take his word *for everything*?

He'd reassured her that he would be faithful, but then he would have, wouldn't he? It would be in his interest to tell her what he knew she would want to hear.

But she had seen what she had seen and if her interpretation had been off target, then he wouldn't be standing there in front of her now, still as a statue, with eyes as cool as an Arctic blast, expecting her to just blindly believe him. He would be defending himself.

She shoved the priceless diamond at him.

'I can't go through with this. I'm sorry. When Dad comes, we'll leave. Right now, I'm going to pack my bags, and don't worry. I won't be taking anything I didn't come here with.'

CHAPTER TEN

WOULD SHE SKULK out of the house? Slip back into her jeans and tee shirt? Shimmy away from the clutter of guests, excitedly sipping their expensive drinks and tucking into expensive canapés and exchanging notes on what had happened since the last annual charity gala had brought them together?

Everyone in the neighbouring towns would be there, from the great and the good to those way down the pecking order. No discrimination, as Luca had told her with some satisfaction a few days previously, when she had been fretting about it.

She shuddered when she thought about running away. The guests would not have started arriving if her father arrived on time but if his flight was delayed, then she ran the risk of doing a runner in the most awkward of situations.

How on earth was Luca going to deal with it? What would he say?

She closed her mind off to any weakness and focused on flinging clothes into her suitcase, the one she had brought with her.

When everything was packed, she stood back, breathing hard, and stared at her reflection in the mirror. She didn't see herself. Instead, she saw Luca in that darkened office with his arms around Isabella, comforting her, his face soft with affection.

Without stopping to think too hard, she climbed out of the designer dress that had made her feel like a million dollars, and crept back into the loose leggings she had adopted ever since her stomach had started expanding and a baggy white tee shirt.

These were the clothes she belonged in.

She sat on the bed and waited. Eventually, her mobile pinged with a text from her father that he was in the taxi and would be with her in under an hour, at which point she agitatedly paced the room, only emerging to head downstairs when she was sure that he would be about to arrive.

There was no sign of Luca.

She wondered whether he had disappeared back into the office with Isabella. Perhaps he was explaining the situation. Maybe he had decided that he would revert to his original plan and marry the girl he had been destined to marry in the first place. It wouldn't take him long to realise that joint custody worked.

Cordelia didn't think there would be any begging by him for her return. He was a proud man and she couldn't have dented his pride more successfully if she'd spent a year planning it.

The fact that he hadn't bothered to find her said it all.

For a moment, she'd stepped into a world as dazzling as a fairy tale. Her prince had stepped forward and, okay, so it might not have been ideal happy-ever-after material but, deep down, she'd figured that there was enough love inside her for both of them. Deep down, when she looked close enough, she'd flirted with the tantalising hope that, with a ring on his finger and a baby on the way, the love he claimed he could never give her would find a way out.

For all she had told herself that the only way to deal with what was on the table was to apply cold logic and reason, she had still succumbed to the notion that things might change because nothing ever remained the same.

She'd been a fool.

Leaving the suitcase in the bedroom and with no clear plan as to what she would tell her father or how, exactly, she would make her exit, she headed down the stairs, slipped into the sitting room closest to the front door, and waited by the window for the taxi bringing her father to arrive.

She wasn't going to do it. Not really. Surely not. The world would be gathering at the villa in under two hours. There was no way she was going to rock the boat at the eleventh hour. She'd reacted with all the emotionalism he knew her to be capable of but she would cool down.

Wouldn't she?

'Go and find her,' Isabella had urged, her pretty face anxious and distressed.

Luca wasn't going to do any such thing.

She would calm down. At any rate, he refused to go down the road of explaining himself to anyone. Surely it wasn't too much to ask for trust in a relationship? He had told her that there was nothing going on between Isabella and himself and he didn't see why she couldn't take him at his word. Had he ever, since she had shown up, given her any reason to think that he was the sort of guy who couldn't be trusted? No, he had not!

Skewered with uncertainty, Luca thought of her, her open, trusting face clouded with doubt and accusation. Something inside him twisted and, like a dam bursting, thoughts that had been pushed to the side now broke through in a tumultuous rush.

A rapid succession of images darted through his head, images from the very first time he'd laid eyes on her in that little room in the cottage she shared with her father to that mind-blowing moment when they had made love for the first time.

And along with those images came other things, feelings he had stashed away, emotions he had never thought he would have.

Galvanised into action, Luca took the stairs two at a time, up to the bedroom, where he saw her packed suitcase on the bed.

It was small, a relic from her dad's days in all probability. The sight of it made him feel sick.

At least he knew she hadn't left the villa.

Heart hammering, he raced through the rooms, impatiently brushing aside several employees who wanted to talk to him, ask his advice on something or other. He barely noticed the way the house had been transformed. He certainly had no time to stop and make polite noises about all the work that had been put into turning his mansion into a wonderland of lights and candles.

He'd started his search in the vast hall but the room she was in was the last he actually looked in. She was gazing out of the window with her back to the door. She hadn't turned on the light and she was a shadowy figure, perched on the window seat.

For a second, Luca had a vivid image of the girl she must have been over the years, sitting just like that, gazing out of a window, dreaming of adventure.

'Cordelia,' he husked, moving quickly towards her. 'No, please don't turn me away. I've come… you're right…'

Luca, she thought, heart leaping, an instinctive reaction to seeing him, to hearing the deep, velvety tone of his voice.

'What do you want?' She edged away from him

because he'd perched right next to her, crowding her and sending her nervous system into frantic free fall. She wished she'd turned the lights on because it was too dark in the room. It had, somehow, felt more comforting to be in the dark when she had entered the room half an hour previously.

'I've been looking everywhere for you.'

'Forget it.'

'You surprised me. I… I wasn't expecting you… when you walked into my office…'

'So I gathered,' Cordelia said icily. 'As you can see, I don't want to have anything to do with you or this gala. I just want you to leave me alone. Dad is going to be here pretty soon and I shall tell him about the pregnancy and then I intend to get a taxi to the nearest hotel for the night. You want to have fun with your ex? Then, by all means, go ahead, but don't think that I'm going to be hanging around in the background, putting up with unacceptable behaviour. I'm very sorry if this means you're going to have to do what most modern-day couples do who share children but aren't together. You're going to have to arrange visiting rights and get a lawyer to sort out maintenance payments. Apologies for putting you in the terrible position of having to behave like a twenty-first-century man, but that's life.'

'I… I'm sorry, *mi tesoro*.'

'Don't call me that.'

'But it's what you are,' Luca said softly. 'You're my treasure.'

'Don't!' She looked away quickly and made a determined effort to staunch her foolish desire to burst out crying.

'Look at me. Please.'

'Go away, Luca.'

'You think I was doing something in there with Isabella?'

'Why would I think that?' Her voice dripped sarcasm. It hurt. It hurt looking at him and it hurt not looking at him. Everything hurt but she knew that this was a turning point. She had to stick to her guns and walk away or else get lost in a relationship that would eat her up and spit her out.

'What you saw...'

'I don't want to hear.'

'I was comforting her, my darling.' He reached for her hand and, predictably, she snatched her hand away and he couldn't blame her.

He honestly couldn't blame her if she walked away and never looked back. He had lied to her about his identity when they had first met; he had questioned her arrival on his doorstep, immediately suspecting the worst. He had lectured her with monotonous regularity on his inability to give her anything beyond what was demanded by duty. He had held himself aloof when he had known that what she wanted and what she deserved was a guy completely committed to her for all the right reasons.

He had presented her with marriage, a union shorn of all the things that should define it, and he had blithely expected her to fall in line.

And then tonight…

When Luca thought about what she must have felt when she'd walked into that room, he wanted to punch something.

And his reaction when she'd pinned him to the spot? He'd brushed aside her very valid concerns because he hadn't seen why he had to explain himself.

On every level he had laid down the rules and expected her to fall in line because that was what everyone did. What he'd seen in her was an opportunity for getting hurt. He'd fallen for her but, instead of facing up to it, he'd rejected it and pushed her back because he'd been afraid.

How could he now expect her to hear him out and give him one last chance?

Why would she not react the way anyone would react and assume that he was fabricating a story simply to get things back to where he wanted them to be?

Why wouldn't she treat whatever he had to say with the cynicism he so richly deserved?

Luca went from pale to sickly ashen as his mind began running away with possible outcomes.

She'd wanted love and marriage and all that stuff he had spent a lifetime writing off as unreasonable nonsense. It was hers for the taking now, but would she believe him or would it be too little, too late?

'I wouldn't blame you if you refused to listen to a word I have to say,' he told her with wrenching honesty. 'And even if you *did* hear me out, I wouldn't blame you if you sent me packing, but I really... need...to...explain myself.'

'But I thought you *never* explained yourself to anyone, Luca,' Cordelia said coldly. 'I thought that if you said "believe me" it was my duty to ask no more questions.'

'Once upon a time, I may have thought like that. I gave orders and people followed them without question,' Luca said quietly, 'but then I met you and it seems that everything changed. I don't know when and I'm not sure how, I just know that I am not the man I once was.'

'Oh, please.' She turned to look away because she could feel his words dragging her back to a place she didn't want to revisit, but he placed one finger on her chin and tilted her back to look at him and she couldn't resist.

'You are the best thing that ever happened to me and I was an idiot for not realising that sooner.' He looked at her and breathed in deeply. This was foreign territory and he had to grope his way to find the right words. 'I met you and I was a different man with you. I was the man I was meant to be and not the man I had been conditioned into becoming. You freed me, my darling, but I didn't pause to analyse why that had happened or what it meant. I just assumed that I acted differently with you because you didn't know me as the billionaire who could have whatever he wanted. I left but my mind kept returning to you and, again, I never asked myself why. I simply ploughed on because that was what I did and what I'd always done. I faced my destiny and my destiny was to marry Isabella and I didn't question it because…that was how it was.'

Cordelia stiffened. The mention of Isabella was a timely reminder of what she had witnessed and, as if sensing her withdrawal, he leaned forward, his body language imparting a searing sincerity that held her spellbound against her better judgement.

'Then you came. You showed up. In all your stunning glory.'

'Don't, Luca,' she whipped back.

'Don't what?'

'Try to get under my skin again. I've had it with you doing that.'

'You thought you walked in on me sharing something intimate with Isabella and, yes, you did, but not in the way you think. Isabella is gay. I've known that for a long time and that's why the marriage made sense. I didn't believe in love. It wasn't for me. And Isabella wanted the cover of a traditional marriage to hide her sexuality from her parents. Not ideal and I tried to persuade her to come out, but she refused, and I suppose, in a way, the arrangement suited me as it stood.'

He sighed, wondered where doing what was right stopped and doing what was convenient began. The lines had become blurred over time when it came to Isabella. 'She was crying because she'd finally decided to tell her parents so that she could be with her partner of eighteen months. She was a wreck and I was trying to comfort her and tell her that it would be okay. That was the scene you interrupted and I was a fool for not explaining myself immediately, for telling you that you had to trust me. Who the hell did I think I was?'

'Isabella is gay? But you were planning on getting married…'

'And who knows? Maybe we would have if she hadn't met the woman she's in love with. Or maybe, if I hadn't broken it off, the worst would have happened and she would have married me because it would have been what tradition demanded. We would have both been miserable in the end.'

'Luca… I wish you had said something. Told me the situation from the start. You have no idea…what's been going on in my head.'

'Old habits die hard.' He grimaced. 'And besides,' he admitted, 'I might have been forced to recognise what I'd been hiding from myself.'

'What's that?' Cordelia asked breathlessly.

'That I'm in love with you. That you were the woman I have been waiting for all my life.'

Afterwards, everything happened very fast. It was a blur. He loved her. She'd questioned him, of course she had. He could be making it up! But she knew he wasn't because it just wasn't something he would ever make up.

He'd never believed in love, he'd told her. Love had destroyed his father. He had lost his only love and then worse had followed when he had reacted by hurtling from one ghastly and costly mistake to another. And he, Luca, young and grieving the loss of his mother, had been a casualty.

What was there to admire about that lifestyle? Only a fool, Luca had confided, would have chosen to emulate it. Only a fool would have blithely believed in the restorative power of love, having witnessed first hand its ability to destroy.

Not for him, and that was the rule he had lived his life by. He would marry for convenience and that way he would never risk getting hurt.

Every word had been music to her ears.

She had had to pinch herself several times because she couldn't believe that the man she had given her heart to had given his heart back to her, not when she had spent so long bracing herself for just the opposite.

Now, back in the gown but on cloud nine, she

slipped her hand into his and gazed at him at the top of the stairs.

Her father was due any minute. Preparations were well under way. Noise levels had escalated. As she gazed down, she could see that the hall was festive with lights and flowers and the smell of food was wafting through the house, making her mouth water.

'I love you.' She smiled at Luca and reached up to kiss him very lightly on the mouth. 'I feel I've spent my life sitting there by the sea, looking out at a horizon and imagining what might lie beyond it. I never, ever thought that I would find everything I could ever hope for and more.'

'The mermaid who found her legs,' Luca murmured, curving his hand against her cheek. 'Mine for ever.'

His eyes slid past her and he smiled.

'Your father is here,' he said, 'and I'm guessing that the buxom blonde clinging to him is none other than the woman he didn't want around because he was too set in his ways?'

Cordelia stared and then burst out laughing because that was Doris, all right. Her case was bulging and Cordelia could only guess at what outfit might be inside. Doris had never been known for her modesty when it came to dress code.

'I don't believe it,' she breathed as they headed down the stairs. She gave a little wave to her father and braced herself for the conversation that would soon be taking place, although, now, it was a conversation she wouldn't be having with a heavy heart.

'Didn't I say?' Luca murmured into her ear. 'All's well that ends well, wouldn't you agree?'

Yes, she would.

There could be no better endings, in fact. She thought that as she looked down at the softly breathing baby in the basket next to the bed.

Three weeks ago, her contractions had kicked in, sending Luca into frenzied panic, even though he had been as cool as a cucumber as the time for the birth had drawn ever closer, wisely telling her when she should pack her bag for the hospital and assuring her that it was all probably going to be far calmer than she feared.

He had stayed with her for the duration of the ten-hour labour, had even helped to deliver their daughter and had only admitted afterwards that he had been close to passing out several times.

He was the most devoted father Cordelia could have hoped for. Now, she felt his arms around her as he shifted against her, levering himself up to gaze at their daughter, breathing softly in her basket, her tiny hands balled into fists. She had a mop of curly dark hair and was pale gold. She was the most wonderful thing they had ever seen and they never tired of admitting it.

Her father had flown over three days after Giulietta was born, along with Doris, and, after fussing over his granddaughter, he had shyly announced that he and Doris would be joining forces to expand the business.

'When you say *joining forces*...' Cordelia had encouraged and he had gone a deeper shade of scarlet.

'Woman's only gone and proposed,' he'd said gruffly, while Doris had looked at him with such tenderness that Cordelia had wanted to rush over and give her a huge hug.

The solitary man who had spent a lifetime mourning the life that had passed him by was finally waking up and Cordelia couldn't have been happier.

There would be another wedding in three months' time and Luca was already making noises about having a proper honeymoon afterwards. Somewhere hot and sunny, with a private beach, where they could relive good times, specifically the good times that had brought their beautiful baby into the world.

'She's a miracle,' Luca murmured, wrapping his arm around his wife and nestling closer to her. 'In case I haven't mentioned it, you girls are the two most important people in my life.'

'I think you've mentioned it before.' Cordelia smiled. She wriggled until she was facing him and their bodies were pressed against one another.

'Have I mentioned, in that case, that I am already thinking that when it comes to family numbers, four seems a far more rounded number than three?'

Cordelia laughed, eyes gleaming. 'Is that a fact?'

'I never thought I'd hear myself say it, my dearest love, but loving you is the best thing that ever happened to me...'

* * * * *

If you found yourself head-over-heels for
Expecting His Billion-Dollar Scandal
you'll love these other stories
by Cathy Williams!

Marriage Bargain with His Innocent
Shock Marriage for the Powerful Spaniard
The Italian's Christmas Proposition
His Secretary's Nine-Month Notice

Available now

WE HOPE YOU ENJOYED
THIS BOOK FROM
HARLEQUIN
PRESENTS

Escape to exotic locations where passion knows no bounds.

Welcome to the glamorous lives of royals and billionaires, where passion knows no bounds. Be swept into a world of luxury, wealth and exotic locations.

8 NEW BOOKS AVAILABLE EVERY MONTH!

#3829 CLAIMING HIS UNKNOWN SON
Spanish Secret Heirs
by Kim Lawrence
Marisa was the first and last woman Roman Bardales proposed to, and her stark refusal turned his heart to stone. Now he's finally discovered the lasting effects of their encounter: his son! And he's about to stake his claim to his child...

#3830 A FORBIDDEN NIGHT WITH THE HOUSEKEEPER
by Heidi Rice
Maxim Durand can't believe that housekeeper Cara has inherited *his* vineyard. But bartering with the English beauty isn't going to be simple... As their desire explodes into passionate life, the question is: What does Maxim want? His rightful inheritance... or Cara?

#3831 HER WEDDING NIGHT NEGOTIATION
by Chantelle Shaw
Kindhearted Leah Ashbourne's wedding *has* to go ahead to save her mother from ruin. So the collapse of her engagement is a disaster! Until billionaire Marco arrives, needing her help. Leah is ready to negotiate with him—but her price is marriage!

#3832 REVELATIONS OF HIS RUNAWAY BRIDE
by Kali Anthony
From the moment Thea Lambros is forced to walk down the aisle toward Christo Callas, her only thought is escape. But when coolly brilliant Christo interrupts her getaway, Thea meets her electrifying match. Because her new husband unleashes an unexpected fire within her...

YOU CAN FIND MORE INFORMATION ON UPCOMING HARLEQUIN TITLES, FREE EXCERPTS AND MORE AT HARLEQUIN.COM.

HPCNMRB0620

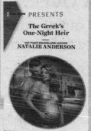

Love Harlequin romance?

DISCOVER.

Be the first to find out about promotions, news and exclusive content!

f Facebook.com/HarlequinBooks

𝕏 Twitter.com/HarlequinBooks

⭕ Instagram.com/HarlequinBooks

𝐏 Pinterest.com/HarlequinBooks

ReaderService.com

EXPLORE.

Sign up for the Harlequin e-newsletter and download a free book from any series at **TryHarlequin.com**

CONNECT.

Join our Harlequin community to share your thoughts and connect with other romance readers! **Facebook.com/groups/HarlequinConnection**

HARLEQUIN

HSOCIAL2020